00 401 048 808

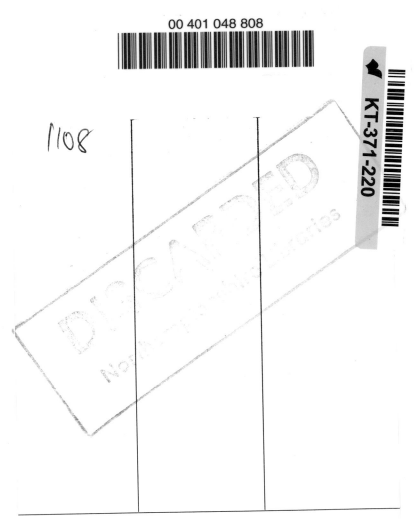

KT-371-220

1108

Please return / renew this item by last
date shown. Books may also be renewed
by phone or the Internet.

Northamptonshire Libraries and Information Service

Northamptonshire
County Council

www.northamptonshire.gov.uk/catalogue

HER MAN IN
MANHATTAN

HER MAN IN MANHATTAN

BY

TRISH WYLIE

All the characters in this book have no existence outside the imagination of the author, and have no relation whatsoever to anyone bearing the same name or names. They are not even distantly inspired by any individual known or unknown to the author, and all the incidents are pure invention.

All Rights Reserved including the right of reproduction in whole or in part in any form. This edition is published by arrangement with Harlequin Enterprises II BV/S.à.r.l. The text of this publication or any part thereof may not be reproduced or transmitted in any form or by any means, electronic or mechanical, including photocopying, recording, storage in an information retrieval system, or otherwise, without the written permission of the publisher.

® and TM are trademarks owned and used by the trademark owner and/or its licensee. Trademarks marked with ® are registered with the United Kingdom Patent Office and/or the Office for Harmonisation in the Internal Market and in other countries.

First published in Great Britain 2012
by Mills & Boon, an imprint of Harlequin (UK) Limited.
Large Print edition 2013
Harlequin (UK) Limited, Eton House,
18-24 Paradise Road, Richmond, Surrey TW9 1SR

© Trish Wylie 2012

ISBN: 978 0 263 23182 3

Harlequin (UK) policy is to use papers that are natural, renewable and recyclable products and made from wood grown in sustainable forests. The logging and manufacturing process conform to the legal environmental regulations of the country of origin.

Printed and bound in Great Britain by CPI Antony Rowe, Chippenham, Wiltshire

Northamptonshire Libraries

CHAPTER ONE

TYLER wasn't the only guy watching her. It was just a shame he didn't want to be there and resented the living hell out of the fact he didn't have a choice.

If things had been different he could enjoy the view.

Pinpricks of sparkling light swirled over the dance floor as she sashayed sideways and made a sexy rotation of her hips. She had a body made for sin: tall, slender, with full breasts and flawless, sun-kissed skin. Raising bared arms above her head lifted the hem of her silver minidress, exposing several more inches of delectably long legs encased in white platform-heeled knee-high boots. Add the sleek bob of a snowy wig, which covered her trademark hair, to darkly made-up eyes and ruby-red lips and she would make a fortune dancing on a dais.

When she bent her knees and shimmied down-wards—rising with an effortlessly fluid curve of her spine—he didn't have difficulty picturing her with a spotlight following her every move. Judging by the fun she'd had fending off potential dance partners she would probably get a kick out of it. But despite her obvious comfort in the centre of so much male attention she stood out of the writhing mass of humanity too much for his liking. She was lucky no one had recognized her and if there was one thing Tyler knew, it was luck had a tendency to run out.

Even for the Irish.

Without warning her gaze collided into his with a pinpoint accuracy, which made it feel as if she'd known he was there all along. The impact created a sudden flare of heat in his body, like a spark igniting a fuse. Refusing to accept it was anything but the natural biological reaction of red-blooded male to hot female, he held his ground and waited to see what she would do next.

Rolling her shoulders and hips, she ran the tip of her tongue over glossy lips and smiled a slow, sensual smile. The silent come-on might have summoned him to the dance floor if he'd ever danced a day in his life. But even if he had he wasn't the kind of guy who came running when a woman crooked an invisible finger. If she wanted to come talk to him she could slide on over. A corner of his mouth lifted.

He was willing to bet she'd be pleased as punch when she found out who she'd been flirting with.

When something was yelled in her ear by her friend she laughed and turned away. A moment later she flashed another smile over her shoulder and swayed, drawing his gaze to the curve of her rear.

Tyler dragged his gaze away. It didn't take a genius to work out she was going to be trouble. He'd known *that* before he laid eyes on her.

Lifting the beer bottle in his hand, he took a long pull and frowned at the label in disgust as he swallowed. Light anything had never been his style; when associated with the word beer it was just all kinds of wrong.

As he experienced a visceral demand from his body to watch her again he forced his gaze elsewhere. Even if he was officially on the clock he wasn't paid to watch her every move. He had to focus on his surroundings; survey the room for potential threats and monitor the crowd. Being attracted to her was a problem he didn't need, especially when it felt as if they'd been tumbling down on him like boulders after a landslide of late.

He missed the days when he had more control over his life. How had it got so screwed up?

When it came to why he was standing there the path was easy to track. A guy had a friendly word of warning for one low life too many and suddenly the brass were tossing around phrases like 'desk duty' and 'temporary leave of absence.' Granted, the fact he was unrepentant probably had something to do with it, but what he still didn't get was why his punishment involved babysitting.

Despite his ability to provide what she was looking for, he had better things to do with his time than spend it reining in an entitled rich kid in search of a few thrills to liven up her—

A familiar face caught his gaze as the music changed to a faster beat and raised an enthusiastic cheer from the crowd. Immediately on alert, Tyler swiftly scanned the rest of the room, targeting two more likely subjects before he hit another face he recognized.

He had to get her out of there.

Setting the bottle down on the nearest table, he looked at the dance floor and frowned when he discovered she wasn't there. Gripping the brass railing in front of him, he played a short game of Where's Waldo? before locating her on her way to the bar with her friend. After checking the nearest exit point, he headed straight for her.

He was two steps away when the music stopped and voices yelled out, '*NYPD. Everyone stay where you are!*'

With her focus on what was happening on the other side of the room, she jumped in surprise as he grabbed her hand. Her eyes widened when she looked up at him. 'What—?'

'This way.'

She tugged against his hold as he dragged her towards the exit. 'Let me go!'

'You want to get arrested?'

'No, but—'

'Then follow my lead.'

Hauling open the door, he stepped them into a dimly lit hallway and looked from side to side. A lightning-fast inventory revealed restrooms, a payphone, steps to what Tyler assumed was a basement on their left and enough banging from the right to indicate they were about to have company. The basement was the most viable option if it had a loading bay that opened onto the sidewalk, but before he could check he heard a crash. Out of time and in need of a distraction, he backed her into the wall and smashed his lips against hers.

Big mistake.

The fuse she'd lit from the dance floor set off the equivalent of an explosive charge. Plumes of fire engulfed him, incinerating rational thought as the invitation of her parted lips was met with the instinctual thrust of his tongue. Need pulsed through his body as an appreciative moan vibrated in her throat. His hand gripped her hip and slid lower. In response she lifted her leg off the ground and hooked it around the back of his knee, allowing him to cradle a silky thigh and lift it higher.

It didn't matter if they were seconds away from being discovered in a highly compromised position. If anything it immediately turned his thoughts to the position his body desperately wanted to be in—his imagination adding fuel to the fire with the suggestion her underwear was as sexy as her dress. Or, better still, non-existent.

'You seeing this?' a voice asked.

'Hey! Break it up over there,' another voice demanded.

Wrenching his mouth free, Tyler hauled in much needed air before squinting at the beams of light aimed their way. Allowing the leg he was holding to lower to the floor he took a step forwards to block her body with his.

'Stay right where you are, buddy,' the first voice said in warning.

Recognizing who it was, Tyler raised his arms at his sides, palms forwards, and waited for the penny to drop with the heavily armed cop. Since silently willing the younger man not to do anything stupid was pointless when saying the words out loud had never had any effect, he added an almost imperceptible shake of his head. When the torch nodded a little he assumed the point had been made and lowered his arms. But when it moved in an attempt to see who was behind him Tyler frowned. 'Problem, Officer?'

'You know there's a raid going on next door?'

'Can't say I'd noticed…'

'We can guess why.' The cop cleared his throat before asking, 'Do we need to search you two for narcotics?'

Funny guy. 'What we're high on doesn't have anything to do with drugs.' Tyler smirked.

A fine-boned hand snaked around his arm and flattened on his chest. 'Can we get arrested for not being able to keep our hands off each other?' the woman behind him asked in a passable, not to mention sultry Southern accent.

Tyler made a note of the fact it obviously wasn't the first time she'd acted her way out of a tricky situation. 'If we can I'm willing to do the time.' He glanced over his shoulder. 'How about you?'

'Are there co-ed jails in the state of New York?' She chuckled throatily, the sound strumming across the taut strings of his libido. 'Just think how much fun we could have sharing a room.'

When she gently caught his ear lobe between her teeth and touched it with the wet tip of her tongue, he felt the impact of the contact all the way to his toes.

'Getting a room *somewhere* sounds like a plan to me,' the officer in front of them said before he lowered his torch. 'Get outta here before I change my mind.'

Grasping hold of the hand on his chest, Tyler headed down the hall and through the busted door. As they entered an alley bathed in flashing red and blue lights one of the cops by a line of vehicles lowered his hand from the radio on his shoulder and waved them through. If he'd been her, he would have had questions about the ease of their escape, but apparently she was too busy jogging on her platform heels to keep up with his determined stride to ask.

'My friend—'

'Unless she's carrying drugs she'll be fine.'

When she tripped he simply tugged on her hand and kept walking, the anger he felt directed as much at himself as her. He could still taste her on his lips: a combination of strawberries, spice and liberation. He couldn't remember a time he'd wanted a woman so badly he would have risked everything for a brief moment of mutual release. What he *could* remember were the days when his timing—not to mention his judgment—had been better.

'Where are we going?' she asked a little breathlessly as they rounded a corner onto a wide street where they stood a better chance of finding a cab.

If she'd been any other woman who reacted the way she had when he kissed her, they'd be headed straight for his place. But he couldn't use her to make him feel good for a few hours even if he made certain she felt the same way. Until he completed his assignment, went back to where he was supposed to be and handed out some justice, he didn't have the right to live his life as if nothing had happened.

To focus his mind he summoned the memory of another woman's face and the words he'd said to her. *'I won't let anything happen to you,'* he'd lied. *'You can trust me.'*

'I'm not taking you anywhere.' When he spotted a flash of yellow he raised an arm in the air to flag down the cab. 'He is.' Digging in his pocket for a handful of bills as the vehicle drew to a halt beside the kerb, he handed them through the window to the driver. 'That should cover it.'

He held open the rear door and waited for her to get inside, his gaze lowered to watch long legs fold gracefully into place before he looked into the shadows of her eyes.

'I don't get a name?' she asked.

'You already have one.'

Her mouth curved into a smile. 'I meant *your* name.'

Tyler shook his head at the liquid cadence of her voice. Next she'd be asking for a phone number and when she could see him again. It was all just one big game to her. He could have been anyone—drug dealer, kidnapper, serial killer—she had no idea how dark the world could be.

But he did.

'You're welcome.' He closed the door and turned away without mentioning she'd be seeing him again real soon.

Why ruin the surprise?

Since it was the last one she'd have in a while, he hoped she'd enjoyed her little adventure. Come Monday she would be playing by *his* rules.

Cross him and he'd make her sorry they ever met.

CHAPTER TWO

AFTER checking that Crystal made it out of the nightclub okay and apologizing profusely for abandoning her, Miranda spent the rest of the weekend fantasizing about her rescuer.

She'd felt his gaze on her before she saw him, which was rare for someone who had spent most of her life being watched. Understandably curious she'd sought him out, her breath catching when she laid eyes on him.

He was the most compelling man she'd ever seen.

From what she could tell he was handsome in a rough-edged kind of way, but that wasn't what made him exciting. What *did* was that even while standing tall and straight he gave the impression of a predator crouched to spring on its prey. Brazenly answering his interest in her with a smile of encouragement had felt like playing with fire, the associated rush of adrenaline addictive.

And when it came to that kiss, *oh, my...*

Smoothing her palms over her elegantly tailored linen dress, she followed the curve from breast to waist to hip. She closed her eyes and allowed herself to imagine the hands touching her body were larger and more masculine; a deep voice was rumbling in her ear, describing everything he was going to do to her in explicit detail.

A sigh of regret left her lips.

If they hadn't been interrupted…

None of her small acts of rebellion had ever given her the same rush she got when she thought about doing more than kissing him. But how would she find him again in a city the size of New York when she didn't know his name?

A familiar three-tapped knock on her bedroom door snapped her out of her reverie.

'Come in,' she called as she stepped over to sit on the stool in front of her dressing table.

'Good morning, Miranda.'

'Good morning, Grace,' she answered cheerfully when her father's personal assistant appeared. 'Isn't it a beautiful morning? The park looks lovely from the windows. I don't suppose there's enough of a gap in my schedule today to allow for a leisurely stroll?'

'No.' Grace's reflection smiled apologetically. 'But at least you'll be outside for a while.'

'Well, that's something.'

While Miranda attached small pearl-drop ear-rings to her lobes, the ever efficient fifty-some-thing who had been in her life for so long she'd become a kind of maiden aunt opened her file and got down to business.

'You have a nine a.m. appointment for a dress fitting with Ms Wang. At ten you're due at a community project in the Bronx with time for a meet-and-greet before morning coffee. At eleven-thirty—'

'Do you think the world would come to an end if we took a day off?' Miranda mused as she added a flawless string of pearls to her neck and fluffed her hair into place. 'We could pack a picnic, grab a handful of gossip magazines and spend the morning people watching...'

When she nodded enthusiastically in the mir-ror Grace closed her file. 'Before or after you go through the Help Wanted ads with me?'

'One little day,' Miranda cajoled with a pout and a flutter of long lashes.

'Your father would like to see you before you leave.'

'Ten bucks says it's a reminder to kiss babies.'

'I don't think they're eligible to vote.'

'No. But with any luck they'll have fathers there

for me to flirt with or mothers for me to charm with talk of how much I want kids of my own one day.' Pushing to her feet, she lifted her bag and shoes and linked their arms at the elbows as they crossed the room.

It was the kind of simple human contact she didn't stop to think about with Grace. She'd heard somewhere people needed eighteen inches of personal space but for most of Miranda's life the distance had been greater. Hence a small part of why the memory of full bodily contact with a virile male was so hard to shake, most likely.

Not that there weren't other reasons.

'It's remiss of me not to have produced a suitable grandchild by now,' she continued in the same bright tone. 'Chubby toddlers are always a hit with the electorate.'

'If you start planning ahead you could schedule it for the whispered campaign for Governor.'

'Always best to keep something in reserve.' Miranda nodded in agreement. She smiled as they stepped into the hall. 'Good morning, Roger. Is that a new tie?'

'Wife bought it for my birthday,' her father's press secretary replied with an answering smile.

'She has excellent taste.'

'Speaking of spouses, finding a husband before

you have that chubby toddler might be a good idea,' Grace whispered conspiratorially.

Miranda leaned closer to whisper back, 'I've heard you don't have to have one to get the other.'

'You do when your father's the mayor.'

Another face in the hallway earned another smile. 'Good morning, Lou. How was the Little League game?'

'Two strikes and a home run,' her father's head of security replied with the swing of an invisible bat.

'Tell Tommy I said *"yay,"'* she replied with a ladylike punch to the air.

'Shoes,' Grace reminded her outside the door to her father's study.

'What would I do without you?'

'Run barefoot and be late for appointments.'

'Now doesn't that sound like fun?' She handed over her bag for safekeeping, slipped on her heels and took a step back to turn a circle. 'Am I ready for inspection?'

'You'll do.'

After a light knock on the door, she waited for the cursory 'come' and turned the handle.

'Ah, here she is,' her father said from behind his mahogany desk as she crossed the room. 'Miranda, this is Detective Brannigan. He'll be overseeing your security during the remainder of the campaign.'

Though unaware there were any changes planned, she kept a smile in place as she waited for the man to stand up and turn around. Her first impression was of his size; he was six feet two, possibly three, his build more running back than linebacker. Many people would have been surprised by that—when they thought bodyguard they pictured brute force—but while physical strength and fitness were both important the members of her family's protective details came in many shapes and sizes. Keen observation skills and an ability to think on their feet were of equal importance.

Any following thought on the subject disappeared in a flash and was instantly replaced by shock when she looked into cobalt-blue eyes. It took every ounce of her social skills to prevent the drop of her jaw.

'Miss Kravitz,' he said in a low rumbling baritone as her hand was engulfed in a firm handshake.

It wasn't what she'd fantasized he would say if they met again but the sound of his voice was enough to remind her of every imagined word. She peeled her tongue off the roof of her mouth as heat suffused her palm and rushed up her arm. Had he known who she was when he came to her rescue? Had he been watching her because he was on duty? How long had he been following her?

As she remembered to reclaim her hand and lowered it to her side—his touch still tingling on her skin—her gaze shifted to her father. There was no way to determine how much trouble she was in while he was wearing his elected official expression but if he was upset about something it was a new tactic. Usually the punishment for her supposed misdemeanors involved a lecture on responsibility—the kind she liked to think she'd endured stoically over the years.

'He'll report to Lou the same way Ron did,' he said. 'They've selected a new detail for you.'

All of her guys had been replaced—since when and, more to the point, *why?*

'Detective Brannigan suggested a shake-up,' he added so she knew who to blame.

While he turned his attention to some of the papers on his desk she looked at the man beside her to see if the reality lived up to her fantasy. Strong masculine features—short, dark blond hair, thick lashes framing his intense eyes. He was every bit as compelling as she remembered. Seeing him again reawakened the potent sensual awareness in her body. It transported her back in time to when he'd kissed her into a boneless puddle of lust and walked away.

Now she thought about it Miranda wasn't certain she'd forgiven him for that. Particularly when it was more than obvious he still had the upper hand. She'd wondered how he managed to get them past a cordon of New York's finest with such ease. In her furtive imagination he'd been everything from a mafia don with cops on his payroll to a combination of secretive billionaire by day and caped crusader by night. That he was *with* the NYPD made more sense but why hadn't he said so? Why the charade? Why kiss her instead of flashing a badge?

He blinked lazily hooded eyes. 'I believe you have a nine a.m. appointment.'

Miranda ignored him and rounded the desk to place a kiss on her father's cheek. 'Bye, Daddy.'

'Bye sweetheart. Have a good day.'

'You, too,' she replied before lifting her chin as she walked back across the room. '*Now* we can leave.'

In a few long strides he'd overtaken her and held open the door but she didn't thank him for the courtesy while she was piqued by his duplicity.

'New bodyguard?' Grace whispered as she

handed over her bag and a copy of the day's itinerary.

Miranda crinkled her nose in mock delight. *'Lucky me.'*

She led the way down the second-floor landing, past a rare five-seat settee that had been discovered in the basement of City Hall. Despite living in the mansion for the two terms her father had been mayor she never took her surroundings for granted. If anything the combination of rare paintings and antiques interspersed with modern furniture reminded her of what a privilege it was to live in one of the few surviving eighteenth-century mansions in the city. It was something she could appreciate more approaching twenty-five than she had at seventeen. But unlike most mornings she didn't take the time to greet any of her favorite pieces with a smile or to mull over her continuing need to escape such a beautifully gilded cage.

She was too distracted by the man walking behind her, her body highly tuned to his presence.

They were halfway down the carpeted stairs before she lowered her voice to ask, 'Did you know who I was?'

'Yes.'

'Did my father order you to follow me?'

'No.'

She smiled at the woman making her way upstairs. 'Good morning, Dorothy. Is it as beautiful outside as it looks through the window?'

'It is,' the maid replied with an answering smile.

The tension became heavier with each muted downward step while Miranda tried to pretend she couldn't feel an intense gaze following her every move. There was no way she could spend every day in the company of a man she'd pictured naked…and sweaty…and as aroused as he'd left her after one little kiss. She had a reputation for being cool, calm and poised in public. She wasn't about to exchange it for hot, bothered and sexually frustrated. It wasn't as if the discovery he was—*technically speaking*—a 'good guy' had done anything to dilute her fantasy, either. Even while wearing a dark suit, white shirt and patriotically striped tie he oozed the danger she'd craved since her late teens.

Skydiving, bungee jumping, swimming with sharks—they were all on an ever-growing wish list of forbidden pursuits she'd added to over the years.

Making wild, crazy whoopee with one of her bodyguards had never crossed her mind, *until now.*

Her heels clicked on the exquisitely refurbished faux marble patterning of the wooden floor in the foyer. In a matter of seconds they would be in the vestibule, away from the constantly moving crowd that never quite managed to make her feel less alone. They could take advantage of the moment and pick up where they'd left off. He would grab her hand and swing her around, press her against the wall with his muscled body, crush her lips beneath his and…

Miranda gave herself a mental smack upside the head. She needed to focus. The brief alone time they had between inner and outer doors should be used to reclaim some of the control over her life she couldn't afford to relinquish. She hadn't been fighting for her freedom so someone new could stride in and clip her wings before she had a chance to stretch them. With that in mind, the second the first door closed behind them she turned to face him.

'As it's your first day I think we should lay out some ground rules….'

'I agree.' He nodded. 'So shut up and listen.'

Miranda gaped at him in disbelief. 'You can't talk to me like that.'

'What you mean is no one else ever has, right?' He didn't wait for an answer. 'I'm willing to bet folks have been kowtowing to you since you were in diapers.' The forwards step he took seemed to suck all the air out of the vestibule. 'What you need to learn quick-smart is I don't kowtow to anyone,' he said in a low, mesmerizing rumble. 'I'm here to do a job. Make that more difficult for me than it needs to be, things will get ugly.' He jerked his brows. 'You feel me?'

Did she—? She blinked. 'I beg your pardon?'

'No begging necessary,' he replied with a small shake of his head. 'Just be a good girl and do as you're told and we'll be golden.'

'You know I can have you removed from this position?'

'Good luck with that. I've been trying to get out of it for a week.' He reached past her, held open the outer door and inclined his head. 'After you, princess.'

A dazed Miranda stepped through the door, her gaze locked on broad shoulders as he overtook her on the gravel driveway. While there was no denying part of her buzzed with the titillating after-effects of his forceful tone, another was mildly outraged. No one had ever spoken to her that way. Who did he think he was?

She narrowed her eyes. It didn't matter who he was. He was about to discover she wouldn't be easily intimidated. She was a politician's daughter. Everything she needed to know about hiding her emotions she'd learned from masters of disguising how they felt. Summoning an air of poise, she reached into her bag for a pair of oversize sunglasses and her cell phone. If he thought he was dealing with a spoilt princess she would give him exactly what he expected. Covering her eyes, she hit speed dial.

'Good morning, darling, how are you?' She purposefully spoke loud enough to be overheard. 'My day has got off to the most *dreadful* start.'

'The Queen of England called and said she wanted her accent back?' Crystal sighed dramatically. 'You're standing me up for lunch, aren't you?'

Miranda smiled smoothly. 'Absolutely not.'

It didn't matter if he was a walking sex fantasy. She planned on ditching her new bodyguard by noon.

CHAPTER THREE

'I ASSUME Detective isn't your first name.'

Tyler glanced in the rear-view mirror. She'd given him the silent treatment since they left the mayor's residence and he'd have been happy for it to stay that way. He wasn't there to make small talk. He was there to keep her safe and out of trouble; something the guys on her previous detail could have done with remembering more often.

'I'll ask Lou,' her honeyed voice said in a dismissive tone when he didn't reply. 'He's a sweetheart.'

Somehow Tyler doubted she'd think so if she knew the mayor's head of security was a big part of the reason he was there. It had been Lou Mitchell's bright idea to draft in someone who hadn't been doing the job for so long they took things for granted or was easily distracted by a pretty face. That Tyler wasn't prepared to be subtle didn't seem to be a problem, which was just as well considering where he'd been drafted *from*.

The next time he glanced in the mirror she'd placed her sunglasses on top of her head and was idly twirling a lock of hair as she read the screen of her BlackBerry. She might have been hot while wearing a disguise but without one she was a stone-cold knockout. Her skin-coloured dress left little to the imagination even with a demure neckline and its hem a respectable couple of inches above her knees. Fitted the way it was—to lovingly follow every curve of her damn-near-perfect body—it had drawn his gaze to her more often than he should have allowed.

The hair she was toying with was a particular source of fascination: lustrous, tumbling tresses of flame blended with sunlight. He could have said his interest in it stemmed from curiosity—how had she got that much hair under a short wig?—but he'd have been lying. The truth was he didn't know why he found it so fascinating. He just did.

But the packaging didn't make up for her personality.

A few hours of watching her in action was all it took to confirm what he'd already suspected. What surprised him was how easily she fooled everyone else. When they got to the second hit of the day and she stepped into a community project for the elderly she pulled out all the stops. A flash of her hundred-watt smile, a few carefully chosen sound bites, the brush of elegant hands over selected arms and she was treated like a combination of visiting European royalty and prodigal granddaughter. By the time she left he suspected there wasn't anyone she came into contact with who didn't believe she genuinely cared what they had to say.

The folks out in Hollywood earned a gold statue for that kind of performance.

His next glance in the mirror revealed she'd shifted her attention from her hair to the pearls around her neck. The fine-boned forefinger tracing them stilled and then she blinked darkened lashes, her hazel-eyed gaze crashing into his before he returned his attention to the road.

'What was your last assignment?' she enquired after another moment of silence.

'You want a copy of my CV so you can get your friend Lou to pull my jacket?'

'Your jacket?'

'My file.' He made a turn and merged the Escalade into three lanes of busy traffic when he heard a sound. 'What are you doing?'

'It's unusually stuffy in here.'

'That's why they invented air-con.' Reaching forwards to hit the switch, he frowned when he glanced in the mirror and discovered she was leaning her face towards the open window. 'And that glass is tinted for a reason.'

'As disappointing as I'm sure it is for you,' she replied haughtily, 'I'm not high on anyone's hit list.'

'You've never read any of the letters that land at your father's office, have you?' Tyler hit another switch to slide the window shut and waited for the answer he already knew.

'We have people who do that.'

'Course you do,' he said dryly while he steered into the middle lane of traffic on Fifth Avenue.

When he drew to a smooth halt at a crossing there was a gasp from the rear seat. 'What a gorgeous dress!'

Though he'd been ready for her to try something the sound of a door being opened caught him off guard. He turned around in his seat. 'Don't get out of—'

Too late. She smiled brightly as she grabbed her bag. 'I'll meet you back here in an hour.' Next thing he knew the door slammed and she was skipping her light-footed way to the sidewalk.

Tyler's seat belt was unbuckled when the light changed, the honking of horns forcing him to ram the Escalade back into gear. With one eye on the traffic and another on where she was headed, he cut across a lane and swung around the corner. It might have taken five minutes of screeching tyres to get there but by the time she exited the rear of the store he was casually leaning against the side of the vehicle with his arms crossed.

The victorious smile on her face faded the instant she saw him. 'How did you—?'

'Clue's in the word *detective*.' He pushed upright and opened the rear door. As she reached him he swung it shut in her face. 'Which part of our talk this morning wasn't clear to you?'

She angled her chin and looked him straight in the eye. 'Which part of your job description suggested you were the boss in this relationship?'

'Who exactly is it you think I work for?'

'You're *my* bodyguard.'

'The city pays my wage.'

'Is there a bonus for being a pain in the ass?' She smiled sweetly.

'Where were you going?'

'That's none of your business.'

'Yeah, it is.' He reached into his pocket for a folded piece of paper and held it up in front of her face. '"Cos if it's not on here, you don't get to go there….'

'It's a free country. I can go where I want.'

Tyler wondered how much effort it had taken not to stamp her foot. 'Let's check the schedule, shall we?'

She crossed her arms as he shrugged back the sleeve of his jacket to consult his watch. 'Eleven fifty-seven.' He glanced over the sheet of paper and shook his head. 'Nope, can't see anything on here about playing hide-and-seek. Maybe yours is different from mine.' His gaze locked with hers again. 'Since we've established other people do the reading for you, maybe I should check that one, too.'

'You carry a gun, right?' she asked with a completely deadpan expression.

Two as it happened but she didn't need to know that. 'You gonna make me use it?'

'I was going to ask if I can borrow it.'

Drawing in a long breath, Tyler refolded the paper and put it back in his pocket. 'If I were you I wouldn't waste time thinking up ways to cut me loose. This is strike one. Three strikes and you won't get to visit a restroom alone.'

'Your last assignment was at Guantanamo, wasn't it?'

The old Tyler might have laughed at the comment. The one standing in front of her simply leaned closer and informed her, 'I'm in your life now. Get used to it.'

The flecks of gold that flared in her eyes hinted at a temper to match her hair. For a split second he wanted her to get mad enough to swing for him—to spit fire and passion and remind him of the woman he'd kissed.

As if sensing a weakness ripe for exploitation she switched tactics. The curve of her full lips became sinful, drawing his gaze to her mouth and calling him to taste her again. She slowly ran the tip of her tongue over the surface, leaving a hypnotically glossy sheen in its wake.

In an instant he remembered how she'd felt when her body was melded to his, how soft her skin had been beneath his fingertips and how badly he'd burned for her. Just as suddenly he was aware of how close they were standing. One more step and their bodies would be touching again.

It took almost as much effort not to frown at his reaction as it did to snap his gaze back up to her eyes. 'That won't work either, so you can forget it.'

'I have no idea what you mean.'

Sure she didn't. He reached for the door handle and jerked his chin. 'Back up a step.'

The order was met with a defiant lack of movement, her luminous eyes narrowed in thought. 'Is my father aware of how you got me out of the nightclub?'

Tyler's arm dropped. He'd wondered how long it would take for her to go there but if she thought she could use it against him, she was wrong. 'You want to tell him where you were?'

'He doesn't know?'

'I thought the mayor was supposed to know everything that goes on in his city.'

'You didn't answer the question.'

'Didn't I?'

The battle of wills made the air between them crackle and when her gaze briefly flickered to his mouth Tyler knew *that kiss* was as much on her mind as it had been on his. Her awareness of him was in the darkening of her eyes, in the increased rise and fall of her breasts. Any hope he'd had that what happened between them could be blamed on the heat of the moment was gone. But while he'd lost his self-control once he wasn't about to let it happen again.

'You getting in or am I putting you there?'

'You can't manhandle me like a common criminal,' she replied on a note of outrage.

'Try me.'

She glared at him as she took a step back. *'Door.'*

Tyler held it open, unable to resist an incline of his head and a sweep of his arm in invitation. 'Your Highness…'

CHAPTER FOUR

HIS attitude *sucked.*

'What is his problem?' Miranda asked as she paced her bedroom floor with her cell phone glued to her ear.

'He's rude, overbearing and obviously doesn't know his place,' Crystal replied.

'Obviously, but that's not what I meant. It's like I've done something to him way worse than making him open a stupid door.'

'He's *supposed* to open doors.'

'He is.' Miranda agreed. 'It's courteous.'

'It is. And how dare he speak to you that way?'

'I know, right?'

Having allowed her the customary five minutes to rant, Crystal called a halt with 'Can we stop being the mean girls from high school now?'

'Do we have to?'

'Yes,' she replied firmly. 'You were never that girl. Now take a deep breath and tell Auntie Crystal what the real problem is.'

Miranda stopped pacing and dropped heavily onto the end of her bed. 'I don't like him.'

'You liked him on Friday night,' Crystal crooned.

'That's when he wasn't a brick wall standing between me and—'

'All those nasty sex fantasies you had about him over the weekend?'

Flopping back onto the soft covers, Miranda blinked at the ceiling and sighed heavily. 'There are at least three people I could have called who'll tell me what I want to hear right now. And yet I still called *you*. Why is that?'

'I'm your reality check,' she said in a matter-of-fact tone. 'The only reason you don't like him now is because he's switched sides. Up till this morning he was part of your dream to do what— or *who*—you want, whenever you want. Now he's part of the system keeping you in servitude.'

'I hate that,' Miranda admitted reluctantly.

'Of course you do. No one likes to have a sex fantasy ruined by reality. We all prefer to live in hope.'

'I was *really* hopeful,' Miranda said wistfully.

'And I really wanted to hear all the sordid details over lunch,' her best friend complained. 'I can't believe you let this guy outwit you.'

'I still have a few tricks up my sleeve.'

'You learnt from the best.'

'You're a bad influence.'

'I *am,*' Crystal said with pride.

'Which if you recall is part of the reason you're not my father's favourite person.'

'He's just never gonna let that reality-TV-show thing go, is he?' she said in a tone that suggested she'd rolled her eyes. 'You were on camera for like, five seconds.'

'Might have helped if I wasn't dancing on a table at the time.'

'Does he have something against people having fun?'

It was an old debate. One Miranda knew she would never win with Mayor Kravitz. As far as *hizzoner* was concerned Crystal was a publicity nightmare: rich, overindulged, and for a considerable amount of time, out of control. She might since have moved on to a lucrative career of celebrity endorsements but when her fame stemmed from notoriety...

Frankly Miranda found it a little insulting he thought she could be so easily led. If she chose to she could get into trouble all on her lonesome. She didn't need *help*. What she needed was the freedom to do what she wanted without her actions becoming fodder for the gossip hungry.

The thought added to her restlessness. She needed to get out for a while before the walls started to close in. Turning her head on the covers, she checked the alarm clock by her bed. 'I'll be at your door in a half hour.'

'Are you going to rant some more when you get here?'

'Probably,' she admitted.

'Awesome. I'll open the wine. By the time you arrive I should be two glasses more sympathetic to your plight.'

Miranda wriggled upright, tucked her phone into the back pocket of her skinny jeans with some cash and pushed her feet into a waiting pair of deck shoes. Twisting her hair into a ponytail, she grabbed a baseball cap from one drawer and sunglasses from the collection in another. Ready for action she opened her bedroom door and checked the hall. Once she confirmed it was empty her lucky music talisman started playing in her head.

It wouldn't be the first time a combination of wits, observation and an extensive study of spy movies was put to good use. As a result she knew to time her progress downstairs; to wait for the turn of the security cameras to take advantage of blind spots. She also knew the best window of opportunity for escape was at shift-change time, when the security details gathered to hand over the baton. At the foot of the stairs she stopped and held her breath, waiting for the last squeaking footsteps to disappear into the back of the house before she jogged across the foyer.

As usual the kitchen was deserted.

A bubble of exhilaration formed in her chest as she made it to the short hallway at the other side of the room. Tantalizingly close to the exit and secure in the knowledge she had an ally on the gate outside, she allowed the music in her head to become a low rhythm on the tip of her tongue. But as she reached for the handle a loud crunch made her still.

When she turned around Detective Party Pooper was leaning against the larder door with an apple in his hand.

'The *Mission Impossible* theme is appropriate,' he said with his mouth full.

Miranda gritted her teeth. 'What are you doing here?'

'Overtime,' he replied with a nonchalant shrug of broad shoulders. 'Reckoned I'd keep an eye on things till the rest of the new detail is up to speed.'

How diligent of him.

She noted his appearance: the lack of a jacket, the loosened tie below an unbuttoned collar, the rolled up sleeves over tanned muscular forearms. When her pulse sped up she ignored it, refusing to have a physical reaction to his presence when she disliked him so much. Instead she focused on how quickly he'd settled in—standing there as if he owned the place and had been there forever.

'I'm trying to decide if this counts as another strike when you haven't left the building yet.' He nodded firmly. 'I'll get back to you on that.'

When he nudged off the wall and went into the kitchen Miranda fought the need to growl. She hadn't thrown a hissy fit since she was eight and denied a puppy, but it was tempting after a day in his company. Aiming a longing glance at the exit she sighed heavily and retraced her steps. He was standing at the island in the middle of the room when she walked in, casually flipping over the pages of a newspaper.

'No disguise,' he commented without looking at her. 'Means you were going somewhere people know you.' Another page of the newspaper flipped over. 'Narrows it down some...'

Miranda swore she would never kiss another handsome stranger. She'd learned her lesson. They could turn into frogs. Now if her fairy godmother could just drop a bolt of lightning out of the sky and incinerate him, she promised to be a very good girl for a very long time. Even if she'd already been there and felt she'd earned a break.

In the absence of magical intervention she considered the options left open to her. She'd be damned if she was retreating to her bedroom. Neither was she staying for a friendly chat over coffee the way she used to with the members of the team she'd *liked*. Giving him anything resembling an order obviously wasn't going to work and she sincerely doubted any attempt at negotiation would end in anything but a migraine.

'I was going to stretch my legs,' she said when the silence began to bother her.

He shook his head as he turned another page. 'Lying sways you closer to strike two.'

'I'm glad the trust part of this relationship is going so well.'

'Stop treating the guys in this unit like idiots and they might trust you a lot quicker.'

Miranda bristled at the accusation. 'You've been here five minutes. You don't know anything about—'

'How many of them do you reckon you got fired?'

'I…' Miranda faltered and frowned at the hesitation. She hadn't got anyone fired. If she had she would have done something to fix it. 'The body-guards who left the mansion *chose* to leave.'

'Ever ask yourself why?'

She lifted her chin. 'Mac said he missed riding in a squad car.'

She'd liked Mac. He was a straight-up guy. Happily married with a young family, he'd done a lot of community policing when he left the academy and said he wanted to get back to it. They'd joked around about the squad car but when it came down to it he missed being in a position where he could talk to people. She understood that but was sorry to see him go. Unlike *some* people, he'd been really good about letting her make unscheduled stops for shopping or lunch when she needed to take a breather. On his last day she'd given him season tickets for the Giants because he loved football so much. She leaned back against the counter and folded her arms. Detective Smarty-pants knew squat.

'Yeah, those things are a real sweet ride compared to the low-spec models you have parked outside.' His gaze lifted. 'Don't know much about guys and cars, do you?'

'I'm reliably informed there's a little more to your job than the toys which go with it.' She nodded at the gun holstered at his lean waist beside his shield. 'It would be nice to think they don't hand those out to everyone who thinks it's cool to carry one.'

When he studied her more intently the memory of how he'd looked at her in the alley that morning entered her mind. For a second she'd thought he was going to kiss her again. A few hours in his company was all it had taken to dissolve her fantasy. At least she'd *thought* it had. But for that long stretched-out moment—as irritated as she'd been by him—she'd wanted him to kiss her.

He raised his right arm and tossed what was left of the apple through the air. As it dropped neatly into a swing-top trash can at the end of the counter he grabbed his jacket off the countertop. 'Come on, then.'

Miranda's eyes narrowed. 'Where are we going?'

'Said you wanted to go for a walk, didn't you?'

'I don't need your permission.'

'No,' he said in a low voice as he turned towards her. 'But since you don't get to go alone, either I go with you or you go back to your room—*your call.*'

'Even if it's not on the itinerary?'

'Why do you think we stick to that schedule?'

Miranda lifted her gaze to the ceiling. 'Gee,

that's a tough one.' She looked into his eyes again. 'But I'm going to guess it's so I know where I'm supposed to be at certain times of the day.'

'There's another reason.'

She batted her lashes. 'So the people I'm going to see know I'll be there?'

'Try again.'

'So you know where to drive me?' She pouted.

She didn't mention it was the tip of an iceberg that could sink her if she thought about it too much. Every moment of her day was planned to the last detail: when she got up, what she ate for breakfast, the visits she made to places her parents couldn't slot into their busy days. She clawed back control where she could—getting to choose her own wardrobe had certainly been a leap in the right direction—but it wasn't enough any more.

It hadn't been for a long time.

'Every place on that list is checked by an advance.'

Oh, for goodness' sake. How long did he think she'd been doing this? 'They search every room, run any necessary background checks and organize escape routes. When they're happy they brief the security details who in turn plan the route to and from the venue.' She raised a brow. 'Are there bonus points if I can tell you everyone's call sign?'

'Don't take losing well, do you?'

'If I'm about to go for a walk in the park when I want to, how have I lost anything?'

'Guess it depends on whether or not that's where you were headed, doesn't it?' he challenged in return. 'And I didn't say anything about the park. The grounds of the mansion will do.' When she didn't reply he tossed his jacket down. 'But if you don't want to go out…'

'Fine,' she snapped as she turned on her heel and headed back towards the exit. Getting out of the house was better than nothing. 'But don't feel you need to make conversation to pass the time.'

'Just remember if you rabbit it'll be the last time we try this,' his deep voice rumbled in warning behind her.

Miranda looked over her shoulder. 'Rabbit?'

'Run,' he translated as he rolled down a sleeve.

It was as if he spoke a different language. She pushed the door open and stepped outside, the last throes of a humid summer surrendering to the first hints of autumn in the evening air. Where was he *from?*

The silent question opened the floodgate for a string of others. She wanted to know how long he'd been a cop, where he'd been before he transferred to the Municipal Security Section, what age he was, if he had a family.

As she crossed the gravel to the lawn another thought occurred to her. Since the absence of a wedding ring meant nothing she didn't even know if he was single. Asking him would be the obvious solution if he was remotely in the region of forthcoming—the fact she still didn't know his name being a prime example. If she found out he was married she would have several names for him; none of them *nice*.

Ramming the baseball cap onto her head, she frowned beneath the cover of the peak. Considering how much of her mind was occupied by thoughts of him even when he was *right there,* she didn't have a choice. She had to get to know him better. Ordinarily it was something she enjoyed: talking to people, listening to what they had to say and getting small glimpses of lives that were so much freer than hers.

With him it felt different, more necessary to her survival, most likely because the silence was starting to turn her into a crazy person.

She just needed to figure out a way of getting him to start a conversation when she'd told him not to.

Had to pick *now* to follow an order, didn't he?

CHAPTER FIVE

AT FIRST Miranda's pace was rushed, the irritation she felt at his presence obvious, particularly when he walked beside her instead of taking up the more usual position on point or a few steps behind. When she slowed and started to take everything in Tyler studied her reaction as she breathed deep and a small smile formed on her lips.

Either she'd never walked the grounds before or she was up to something. He assumed it was the latter.

Without warning she changed direction and headed for the river, stopping to look from side to side when she got to the railing. After a couple of minutes of the same thing he inevitably asked, 'What are you looking for?'

'Mmm?' she hummed absent-mindedly.

'You're obviously looking for something.' If it was a place to jump in the river and swim to freedom she could forget it.

'Baby seals.'

'What?'

'Baby seals,' she repeated. 'Fuzzy bundles of joy that mummy and daddy seal made together as a token of their love for one another.' When she shot a sparkle-eyed glance at him from beneath the peak of her baseball cap he got the impression she thought she'd won some kind of victory. 'Didn't they teach you about reproduction in high school?'

Like most teenage boys it hadn't been the reproduction of seals he'd been interested in but Tyler didn't say so out loud. Instead he checked the grounds and the river, the water still busy with tugboats and barges. There was no immediate danger but he couldn't relax. Every muscle in his body was wound tight, ready to spring into action at a moment's notice. Without a means of release the tension grew, making him hyper-aware of the smallest details.

The name of the tugboat closest to them—the man standing on the prow of a barge—the water lapping against algae-covered rocks—the way a breeze from the river brushed a loose tendril of flame-red hair against the sensitive skin on her neck. He frowned as it swayed back and forth in a whispered touch that made his fingertips itch.

The ability to store large quantities of miscellaneous information in the back of his head until he needed to call on it was something Tyler had always taken for granted. It allowed him to focus his mind and manage the most immediate tasks. In many ways his brain acted like a computer with several open programs, a dozen others working in the background and plenty of spare memory. If that was the case she was messing with his operating system. Every time his eyes opened an image of her the screen froze.

'They're supposed to be around here somewhere,' she continued. 'There was a picture on Twitter.'

'Right,' he said dryly. He'd never been a Twitter fan but he knew she was popular there. It was the one area he hadn't been allowed to suggest changes.

From a protection standpoint he thought regularly reporting her location to all and sundry was an unnecessary risk. From the perspective of the mayor's press office her online presence was a valuable publicity tool. That they wouldn't budge on the subject still bugged him.

But not as much as all the standing around he'd been doing since he reported for duty.

'I don't think they constitute a breach in security if that's what you're worried about.' She glanced up at him again. 'Isn't it supposed to be dolphins they train to carry explosives?' When he didn't say anything, she leaned an elbow on the railing and turned toward him. 'You don't have a sense of humour, do you?'

'Would it save time if I told you I wasn't here to make friends?'

'I'm shocked,' she replied without batting an eye.

Tyler fought his nature. Normally he gave as good as he got; with a woman who looked the way she did it would probably involve a heavy dose of flirting. He could lay on the charm when he set his mind to it. But even if he hadn't been assigned to the position of babysitter his skills were a little rusty. Hadn't had much call to use them when he was buried in work was the easiest explanation. Hadn't met anyone he wanted to use them on was another.

But there was a reason for that.

When the thought conjured an image of long dark hair and soulful brown eyes it didn't improve his mood.

'That's how you got some of the others to turn a blind eye, isn't it?'

She raised an elegantly arched brow. 'What are we talking about now?'

'Your little adventures…'

'What adventures?'

Tyler cut to the chase. 'I do my homework. There isn't anything I don't know about you.'

There was a melodic burst of dismissive laughter. 'I very much doubt that.'

He summoned the necessary information without missing a beat. 'Miranda Eleanor Kravitz, twenty-four, born in Manhattan, raised in Vermont, moved back to New York prior to your father becoming mayor when you were seventeen.'

'Sixteen,' she corrected. 'Elections are in November.'

'He didn't take up office until January. Your birthday is December fourteenth. You were seventeen.' He picked up where he'd left off before she interrupted. 'You were a straight "A" student in high school, made the honour roll and in the final year took one of the leads in a stage production of *Twelfth Night.*' It was probably where she'd picked up her acting skills. 'Fluent in Spanish and French, studied English literature at NYU. By the time you left you'd danced on a table in a reality TV show and made headlines twice—once when you were caught drunk partying with the same infamous party girl who—'

'Has my bra size made it to Wikipedia yet?'

When the old Tyler made a rare appearance his gaze automatically lowered to the scooped neck of her T-shirt. 'No, but I'm willing to go out on a limb and say you're a—'

'Eyes north, Detective,' she warned in a lower voice.

Irritated he'd stepped over the line again, Tyler snapped his gaze back up. 'The investigation I did before I got here involved more than Googling your name. I talked to every bodyguard assigned to you and know exactly how you roll. There isn't an escape route I haven't plugged or a former cohort who hasn't been reassigned. The guy on the gate tonight is new, too, so you wouldn't have got far. You don't have any friends in the security team any more. What you have is people focused on doing their jobs who'll end up back in uniform if they don't.'

The gold in her eyes flared. 'What is your problem?'

'Until you accept you're not going anywhere without me or one of the other guys on your new detail, it's you.'

'You're not my keeper.'

Tyler stepped around her. 'Well, obviously they figured you needed one or I wouldn't be here.'

'Who are *"they"?*' she asked as she followed him.

'Who do you think they are?'

She muttered something incoherent below her breath but judging by her tone it wasn't a word she'd picked up from a study of English literature.

When he stopped and turned around she took a step back and frowned at the centre of his chest.

'This close to the election you're a liability,' he told her flatly. 'Three weeks back you were photographed sitting on a bar while some random guy licked salt off your neck before taking a shot of tequila.'

She lifted her chin. 'Jealous?'

'Personally I couldn't give a damn what you do.' Even if his reaction to seeing the photographs after he kissed her might have suggested otherwise. 'The only thing that concerns me is making sure it doesn't happen again. Some major favours were called in to keep those pictures out of the public eye.'

Any surprise she felt was hidden behind a mask of ice. 'It's just as well there wasn't anyone with a camera in a darkened hall on Friday night, then, isn't it?'

When she turned on her heel and headed back to the mansion Tyler let her get a few steps ahead. He needed to take a beat. Her parting shot had been bang on target but that wasn't what grated him.

What did was the indifference in her voice. He wasn't the only one who got carried away in that hall. The implication he could have been just another guy lining up to lick salt off her neck bothered him a great deal more than it should.

At a very basic level he wanted to march on over there and demonstrate she was wrong. A Brannigan never backed down from a challenge. Trouble was they were also carved with deep streaks of honour and duty and while he knew how close he was to breaking one code, he had to hang on tight to the other. If he didn't there would be nothing left of the man he was before everything got so messed up.

'Go home, Detective,' she demanded when they were back in the kitchen.

'No can do,' he informed her retreating back.

When she turned he got a brief glimpse of how angry she was from the flash of fire in her eyes. Then the ice returned. 'I'll make a deal with you.'

'What kind of deal?'

'I'll give you my word I'll stay in tonight and that way you won't have to camp outside my door.' She ran an impassive gaze down the length of his body and back up. 'A good night's sleep might help with all the tension you're carrying around…'

Tyler treated her to his patented interrogation

face: the one that said nothing short of a nuclear blast would change his position. 'What's the catch?'

She shook her head. 'No catch.'

'What do you get out of it?'

'Apart from a break from you?'

The thought he got to her went a long way towards evening the playing field, but there was more to it than that. 'You want something.'

'World peace, an end to poverty, freedom and justice for all... I want a great many things, *Detective*. But for now I'll settle for your name.'

What was the big deal with his name? He ran through every possible scam she could be running and came up short. But with his Spidey-senses on alert he knew whatever she was doing was part of something bigger. That was okay, he could play the long game, and if giving her a name was what it took to give him a few hours he could put to better use than standing twiddling his thumbs or sleeping...

'Tyler.'

'Tyler,' she repeated in a lower voice as if savouring how it felt on her tongue.

Hearing her say it had a mesmerizing effect he'd never experienced before. Time stretched inexorably while she stared at him, her chin angled in contemplation. As he tried to figure out why his blood had thickened to the same consistency as magma when she hadn't done anything overtly seductive, she blinked and turned away.

'I'll see you in the morning, Tyler.'

'You leave this house, I'll know inside five seconds.'

She raised an arm and waggled her fingers in the air. 'Nighty-night.'

Tyler stood in the same spot after she left, trying to decide whether he trusted her any further than he could throw her. His word meant something—or at least it used to; he wasn't convinced hers did. Then his cell phone vibrated.

'Brannigan.'

'So what's it like with the city's version of the Secret Service?'

The sound of his partner's voice got him moving again. 'Don't ask,' he said as he left the kitchen and headed for the control room. 'Got anything new for me?'

'There weren't any DNA hits in the database.'

'It took them a month to tell us that?'

'Backed up in the lab…'

'What about the known associates we've been chasing?'

'There I might have better news.'

Tyler nodded brusquely. 'Save it for when I see you. I'll be at O'Malley's by nine.'

'If I end up divorced I'm blaming you.'

'Because all your kids look like me?'

The response made the corner of Tyler's mouth lift. It was the closest he got to a smile any more. Pretending nothing was wrong when he was around the people who knew him was wearing him down. From that point of view his day with the mayor's daughter had been a welcome respite.

He just had to get a handle on his reaction to her while he was still volatile.

There'd been a time when not getting involved had never been a problem for him the way it had for other members of his family. He'd kept his distance and remained detached, gaining a rep for being emotionally unavailable to women along the way. Once he'd made the mistake of thinking he could handle a little attachment he'd fallen flat on his face. To top it off he'd overcompensated and it had cost someone their life.

Sometimes he thought he saw her face in a crowd: dull, lifeless eyes staring at him in silent accusation. She was a ghost who followed him everywhere.

He shouldn't have left her alone.

The thought gave him a moment's pause outside the room that housed the security monitors. From inside he could hear the voices of the men whose presence meant he wasn't leaving the mayor's daughter unprotected even if there was an immediate threat.

There was no reason for him to feel torn.

A small army of people surrounded Miranda Kravitz and, though they might not have kept her out of trouble, they had plenty of practice cushioning her from the world beyond the walls of the mansion. It wasn't as if she didn't have a voice, either. Half her problem with him was he didn't let her get her own way when she was plainly accustomed to getting whatever she wanted.

Tyler stood up for the people who didn't have a voice, who didn't have the opportunities she'd been given or the ability to escape their lives when they felt like it. If she broke her word, she would pay for it. He'd see to that.

She might think he'd been tough on her the first day, but she had no idea how ruthless he could be.

CHAPTER SIX

THE small victories gained when she got him to start a conversation and give her the name she so badly wanted to know were enough to allow Miranda to cut him some slack. She wouldn't break her word. What helped him *more* was that he'd given her somewhere else to focus her ire. After a night of enforced captivity she was determined to fight for her rights.

'Good morning, Miranda.'

'Good morning, Grace.' She saw the surprise in the older woman's eyes when she appeared outside her father's office. 'Is the mayor in?'

'He's having breakfast with the chief of police.'

'Where is my mother?'

'I believe she's still in the morning room.'

When she turned on her heel Grace grabbed her file, rounded her desk and rushed down the hall after her. 'You have a nine a.m. appointment in Brooklyn at—'

'Not now, Grace.' It was rude and she was sorry

for that but they both knew the morning briefing was more habit than necessity. Miranda knew where she was going days in advance—weeks for the functions that required more forwards planning. If she didn't how was she supposed to know what to wear or find time to research things she knew nothing about so she could hold a conversation?

Two sets of eyes looked across the morning room as she entered without knocking. 'Could you give us a moment, please, Roger?' Once the door shut behind him Miranda took a deep breath. 'I won't be held prisoner in this house.'

'Sit down, darling.'

'I don't want to sit down,' she said without moving. 'What I want is to be treated like an adult.'

'Start behaving like one and you will,' her mother replied with the infinite patience that drove her daughter insane when she was upset about something. 'Now take a seat and tell me what's wrong.'

'You knew, didn't you?'

'Knew what?'

'About the changes to my security detail.'

'It's hardly the first change of personnel since we took up residence.' Her mother raised a brow. 'Don't you think you're overreacting a little?'

'When they were brought in specifically to keep me out of trouble in case I prove an embarrassment to you during the campaign?'

'Well, obviously we would prefer to avoid any negative publicity this close to—'

'I'm more than aware of the responsibilities forced on me since my teens, Mother. I don't need a reminder.'

'Yet your father and I are being given increasingly regular reports of your acts of rebellion.' She gracefully folded her hands together on her lap. 'We were elected to set an example. People expect more of this family. That's the life we live.'

'*We* weren't elected,' Miranda reminded her. '*Dad was.* I didn't choose to run for office and I wasn't elected to the position of your daughter. Doesn't the fact I've lived someone else's life for half of mine count for anything?'

'Like it or not, you're still the mayor's daughter. This is his last term in office and—'

'*If* he's elected or are we taking that for granted? Throwing pots of money at the campaign isn't an automatic guarantee of success.'

'We're a family, Miranda. We stick together through everything. Once the election is over—'

A small burst of sarcastic laughter left her lips. 'I'm supposed to do what—wait until he decides whether he wants to confirm the rumours and run for Governor? Why stop there—what about the White House?'

'That's your father's decision.'

'And how I choose to live my life is mine. If you want me to act like a grown-up you have to allow me to be one. How am I supposed to learn from my mistakes if I'm not permitted to make any?'

'Your argument might carry more weight if there was any evidence to support it,' her mother replied. 'We gave you more freedom at NYU and you repaid our trust by having your picture splashed across several tabloids.'

Miranda's frustration grew. 'I love dancing and got drunk when I turned twenty-one—how does that make me worse than any other college student in America? I could have been running around in a wet T-shirt during spring break or got arrested at student protests. I could have experimented with drugs or slept with guys who were happy to make a buck selling all the gory details to the press. I didn't but none of those things matter any more than the long hours I work. Did it occur to either one of you that turning this place into the equivalent of Alcatraz would make the need for escape more necessary? Why do you think Richie chose to attend a college on the other side of the country?'

'There's no need to raise your voice. If you would learn how to state your case calmly and sensibly the way your brother does—'

Miranda shook her head. No matter how often she tried to communicate with her mother every conversation left her feeling like a petulant teenager. The truth was her parents didn't know their son any better than their daughter. While they had disappeared off to countless business meetings, charity benefits and met with people who were keen for her father to launch his political career their daughter had become a surrogate mother.

She'd read her baby brother bedtime stories and made sure he did his homework. She'd put Band-Aids on cuts, watched cartoons when he was sick and held his hand when they'd had to face a world filled with curious eyes.

No one had done those things for her.

'I'm done,' she said flatly. 'I'll stick around for the election but once the votes are counted, I'm out. No more public appearances, no more smiling for photographers and no bodyguards following me everywhere I go. I never wanted one to begin with and I don't see why the taxpayer should suffer because my overprotective parents want to control my every move.'

It meant breaking the pact she'd made with her brother but it couldn't be helped. Not when another eight months felt like a life sentence.

There was a heavy sigh as she turned away. 'Miranda—'

'I'm going to be late for my first appointment.' When she yanked the door open and stepped into the hall her gaze lifted and crashed into cobalt-blue eyes.

Her breath caught. *Tyler.*

With her heart still beating hard as a result of a long-overdue parental confrontation she experienced the same difficulty she had the last time his name echoed in her mind. She couldn't break eye contact, was frozen in place and her brain seemed to have turned into mush.

He broke the spell with the blink of dense lashes and held out a sheet of paper. 'I told Grace I'd make sure you got this.'

'Thank you.' She took the schedule with one hand and closed the door behind her with the other.

'You ready to go?'

'I need a couple of minutes.'

He nodded. 'I'll be outside.'

Miranda turned the sheet of paper in her hands as they walked down the hall. When she stole an upward glance at his profile she saw the corner of his mouth lift.

'Bye, Grace,' his voice rumbled.

'Bye, Tyler.'

Her gaze shifted in time to catch a glimpse of what looked like a hint of warmth on the older woman's cheeks. In all the years she'd known her, she'd never seen Grace blush. Or be flustered enough to feel the need to shuffle the papers on her desk. Had he just winked at her?

The thought was surreal.

When she stole another glance as they approached the top of the stairs he caught her doing it. Adopting the same impassive expression he was wearing, she simply blinked and looked away. If there was one thing she'd learnt about him it was when he had something to say he didn't have any difficulty opening his mouth. Keeping it shut on the subject of anything he might have heard through the door would be her advice.

When he remained silent she lifted the sheet of paper and glanced over her day.

'You need any help with the big words, let me know.'

The comment made her glare at him in warning before they parted ways but as she continued down the hall to her bedroom something unexpected happened: she smiled.

Unwittingly he'd given her exactly what she needed to face the day. Combined with the knowledge that her release date was closer, it placed a spring in her step that hadn't been there before.

CHAPTER SEVEN

SOMETHING was eating at Tyler.

Usually it meant he'd missed something—a random clue or part of the puzzle that didn't quite fit. That Miranda would make another bid for freedom was a given. What he didn't get was why it suddenly felt wrong to stand in her way.

Hearing what he'd heard through the door that morning probably had something to do with it. The knowledge she hadn't wanted a bodyguard helped raise his opinion of her a notch, even if she was under the misconception she didn't need one. But then she didn't know what he knew, did she?

His gaze scanned the room, but with little cause for concern among a bunch of kids and schoolteachers it slid back to his mark. The long legs encased in sharply tailored dark grey trousers were folded elegantly to the side, one high-heeled open-toed white shoe tapping in time to the music while she smiled. Judging by the sparkle in her eyes, she would probably agree calling the recital *music* was a bit of a stretch but it didn't seem to dilute her enjoyment any.

Maybe that was what was eating him: *her mood.*

She'd been Little Miss Sunshine since she appeared outside the mansion.

When the cacophony of sound limped its way to an overly enthusiastic end she led the applause and stood up. 'Thank you, that was wonderful. The mayor would have loved this. If you keep practising and get to Radio City Music Hall I'll make sure he has front-row tickets.'

Tyler doubted there was an adult present who didn't think they would need to be practising for a very long time before that happened. Opening the door, he stepped into the empty hall, inhaling the scent he'd had so much difficulty ignoring on the trip over as she passed within inches of him. It was different from the sophisticated perfume she'd worn the day before. Since he wasn't up to date on flowers he couldn't identify what it had been but now he thought about it he reckoned it was probably something like lilies or lilac. The one she was currently wearing was sweeter, more playful and made him wonder if she matched her perfume to where she was going with as much care as her clothes.

If she did it was clever. Even if he could have

done without the constant trace of strawberries in the air as a reminder of how she'd tasted on his lips.

He followed a few steps behind as the head teacher and members of the board escorted her along the hall. When his gaze lowered to the feminine sway of her hips he hid a frown of annoyance and forced it elsewhere.

'This next class is made up of children with learning difficulties,' the principal explained. 'The ratio of teacher and classroom assistant to pupil is higher.'

'What is the age range?' Miranda asked.

'Between six and eight…'

When they filed inside Tyler took up position by the door again. After a cursory inventory of his surroundings, the occupants and checking the line of sight through the windows there wasn't much else for him to do but continue watching her. He justified the action by telling himself he was searching for the clue he might have missed, examining everything from her introductory wave to how she interacted with the children as she moved from one small desk to the next. She crouched down to eye level, asked questions and listened carefully to the answers. From time to time she ruffled the odd tousled head of hair, her hundred-watt smile flashing more than once.

It wasn't dissimilar to the act she'd put on with the elderly in the Bronx the day before but Tyler couldn't shake the sensation something was different.

As the principal explained some of the ways they made it easier for the kids to stay focused somewhat ironically Miranda's attention wandered. When her gaze landed on something at his side of the room and she angled her chin with curiosity, Tyler looked to see what it was.

A little girl with blonde hair sat on padded mats on the floor a few feet away, seemingly oblivious to what was happening around her as she swapped one thick crayon for another and continued colouring a sheet of paper.

Miranda crossed the room and hunched down beside her.

'Hello.'

The girl didn't look up.

'Would you mind if I sat with you for a minute? My feet are really starting to hurt in these shoes.'

No reply.

Regardless of her expensive outfit, she sat down and tucked her legs to one side. 'That's a very pretty picture. I love the flowers. Pink is my favorite colour.'

After a moment's hesitation the girl reached for a pink crayon, her chin lifting as she held it up.

The gesture was received with an impossibly soft smile. 'Is that for me?'

There was a nod.

'Are you sure you want me to help? I can never stay between the lines when I'm supposed to.'

Tyler thought it was the most honest statement she'd made since they met. That it was said with a hint of self-recrimination was interesting. For a second he almost believed it was a glimpse of the real her.

Accepting the crayon, she brushed her hair over her shoulder and looked at the picture again. 'Which one do you want me to do?' A small finger pointed at the page. 'Okay. I'll try not to mess it up for you.'

Tyler looked at the captivated audience of adults who were watching what she was doing. He doubted any of them would forget it before they cast their vote in the election. They'd see her father's name on the voting slip and think of her. Maybe even tick the box next to his name if they'd been wavering.

He'd thought New Yorkers were savvier than that.

'You have flowers,' a small voice said.

His gaze was drawn back to Miranda as she glanced down at her blouse. 'I like the ruffles and the layers. They all feel different. Try one and see.'

A small hand reached out to one of the larger grey and white flowers pinned randomly to white linen. Catching a ruffle between a thumb and forefinger, the girl checked out how it felt. 'Soft.'

'Do you like the beads in the middle?'

'They're shiny.'

'Someone has to sew them on with a needle and thread.'

'Did you do it?'

'*Nuh-uh,*' Miranda sang in reply. 'Needles are pointy. It's not a good idea to play with the things that might hurt you.'

Something she could have done with remembering before she gave a stranger the come-on from a dance floor.

Tyler looked away and found a boy at a nearby desk staring at his waist with wide eyes. Lightly shrugging his shoulders, he tugged the edges of his jacket closer together to cover his sidearm and checked his watch. It was almost time to leave.

Shifting his gaze to his mark, he waited for an opening to make eye contact.

'What's your name?'

'Casey.'

'I'm Miranda. Why are you sitting on your own, Casey? Don't you want to sit with your friends?'

'There are boys at my table,' she explained with the typically solid reasoning of most small girls her age.

'Some boys can be nice.'

'Some of them are mean.'

'Believe me, *I know.*' Obviously stifling amusement, Miranda shot a pointed glance his way.

Cute—with a lazy blink to indicate he'd got the message, Tyler subtly tapped his watch. *Tick-tock, princess.*

'I have to go now, Casey,' she said with a pout before turning it into a smile. 'But it was very nice to meet you. Thanks for letting me colour with you.'

'Are your feet better?'

'Much better, thank you.' She pushed upright and ran her palms over the seat of her trousers, brows lifting when the sheet of paper was held up in the air. 'I can take it home with me?'

'You can finish it at your house.'

'I will, I promise. Bye, Casey.'

'Bye, Miranda.'

She waved to the rest of the room. 'Bye, kids. Thanks for letting me come visit you today. I can't wait to tell the mayor how great you're all doing in school.'

Tyler stepped into the hall as there was a chorus of goodbyes. Lifting the mike in his closed hand, he spoke into it in a low voice.

'Rand from Brannigan, Phoenix is on the move.'

The reply sounded in his earpiece. 'Roger that— moving to primary.'

As they approached the main entrance Tyler tuned out of the conversation and went on alert. There had been a small gathering of parents outside when they arrived, but, taking into consideration how long they'd been there, the numbers might have grown. When the group in front of him stopped in the foyer he headed for the doors to check it out. What he discovered made him twice as determined to stay focused. He had to hand it to her: whatever else she might be, the woman was a crowd-puller.

When she said her goodbyes, shook hands and headed his way he stepped outside, his eyes on the crowd as he walked a few feet in front of her. What he was looking for as she approached the people yelling for attention was someone who stood out, whose actions and demeanor were different from everyone else's. While she waved and stopped to shake hands on the approach to Officer Rand at the waiting Suburban, Tyler took dozens of mental snapshots. A couple of minutes and an alarm bell went off in his head.

He went back over the last faces he'd seen while she talked to a young woman who followed her on Twitter.

At the back of the crowd there was a man who wasn't smiling or yelling. He was pale and ordinary looking, the kind of guy who normally faded into the background. Dark hair, approximately five feet eight, glasses, baseball cap with a faded lion logo—nothing unusual there. What made him stand out was how he was fixated on Miranda as if she was the only thing he could see.

Suddenly Tyler was aware of every hand reaching out for her, the weight of bodies pressed against the barricade close to where she stood and the flapping greeting banners that could obscure any of the danger behind them.

Adrenaline sped through his veins while his gaze flickered to face after face. With a sickening sense of inevitability heads moved in the crowd and he saw the one face he would never forget. Dull, lifeless eyes filled with accusation stared at him from a face streaked with blood.

It didn't matter that the man at the back of the crowd hadn't moved. He couldn't take a chance.

Stepping towards Miranda, he laid a palm on the inward curve of her spine and leaned close to her ear. 'You need to go now.'

Her body stiffened as she looked into his eyes. 'Why?'

'Just do it.' He added pressure to her spine to move her along.

To her credit she dealt with the situation a lot better than he did, smiling brightly and waving goodbye as he ushered her to safety. If he had time to stop and think about it Tyler might have realized he respected her for that. But since he was too busy getting her the hell out of there he jerked his chin at Rand, who opened the rear door and looked around.

'Problem?' he asked when Miranda was inside.

'Guy on my six at the back of the crowd.'

Rand looked over his shoulder. 'Which one?'

'Pale complexion, glasses, baseball cap.'

'Don't see him.'

Turning ninety degrees and zeroing in on the

position, Tyler frowned when he discovered the man wasn't there.

'Let's go.'

'What's wrong?' Miranda asked when he opened the driver's door and got behind the wheel.

He watched Rand through the windscreen as he walked around the front of the vehicle to the jump seat. 'Nothing you need to worry about.'

'Nice try.' To his surprise her voice softened. 'I saw your face, Tyler, and—'

'We have a schedule to stick to,' he said tightly as the passenger door opened. When their gazes met in the mirror something resembling under-standing passed silently between them before she glanced at Rand.

She shook her head. 'You're more obsessed with my schedule than Grace.'

It wasn't the first time she'd followed his lead. But that she hadn't pushed on the subject in front of his fellow officer made it feel as if *she* was pro-tecting *him,* which was not a pleasant sensation for Tyler. Pulling away from the kerb, he headed them back to Manhattan and took deep, even breaths. That his heart rate still hadn't returned to normal by the time they got to the Brooklyn Bridge wasn't unusual—he'd been in plenty of situations where adrenalin continued to course through his body long after the event.

But this time felt different.

He just wasn't sure he wanted to know why.

CHAPTER EIGHT

As SOMEONE who'd been looking forwards to a little one-on-one time with her new prison warden—albeit in the form of a continuing game of one-upmanship—Miranda found the addition of a second bodyguard a tad frustrating. By mid-afternoon she was glad to see Lewis go, especially when she hadn't been able to get what happened off her mind. They'd barely left the civic reception at City Hall before she focused on what she could see of his reflection in the rear-view mirror and broached the subject with Tyler.

'What happened this morning?'

'I told you it was nothing to worry about.'

She scowled at his eyes when they didn't look at her. The fact he was driving through heavy traffic didn't seem to matter. 'I didn't push the subject when Lewis was here,' she reminded him. 'But I saw the look on your face and there's no way you were that spooked about nothing.'

'I wasn't *spooked.*'

'Call it what you want, I know what I saw.'

The atmosphere within the cocoon of the SUV grew darker, the lack of a response adding to her frustration. 'The whole mean, moody and mysterious thing you're working so well won't cut it with me. If you want to build a level of trust in this relationship it has to go both ways.'

'When I think you need to know something, you will.'

She tried to figure out why she'd wasted time worrying about him. Despite his denial he'd been spooked, Miranda couldn't think of a better word to describe his reaction. When she'd stolen a glance at him as he watched the crowd he was frozen in place, ramrod straight and the colour seemed to have faded beneath his tan.

Momentarily distracted by the conversation she was having with the person closest to her, she hadn't seen him move. She could still feel the pressure of his large hand on her spine, the heat of his touch branding her through the material of her blouse as an electric current zinged through her body. Adding the deep rumble of his voice so close to her ear she could almost feel his lips move left her skin feeling several sizes too small to fit over her bones. He would never know how much effort it had taken to make it look as if she hadn't been so shaken by it she wouldn't have noticed if the sky had fallen down.

As she turned her head and looked out of the side window she blamed her fantasies. The time she'd spent dreaming about having seriously hot sex with him combined with the forbidden aspect of physical contact with one of her bodyguards had left her body primed in a way it had never been for any other man.

The pang of hurt she felt was harder to justify.

When she'd looked into his eyes in the mirror, she'd thought she felt a flicker of understanding pass between them and dropped the subject until they were alone. It was the same way she'd felt in the school when she teased him about being mean and even made her wonder if giving her what she'd needed after the confrontation with her mother had been unintentional.

She wouldn't make the same mistake again.

By rejecting the olive branch she'd offered him, Detective Brannigan had sealed his fate.

Fishing in her Herrera bag for a pair of sunglasses, she hid behind them while she plotted her revenge.

CHAPTER NINE

LIKE every other guy on the planet Tyler could think of a million other things he would rather do than sit around waiting while a woman went shopping for clothes. That she felt the need to parade each outfit in front of him wasn't helping any, especially when it gave him an excuse to fill his mind with image after image of her body.

Leaning forwards on a velvet-covered chair, he rested his elbows on his knees, staring at the cream carpet while he crossed his jaw and mentally prepared for the next test of his self-control.

'This neckline might be a little too low,' her voice announced from beyond the curtain.

While he appreciated the warning he still felt the need to take a deep breath and blow it into his cheeks before exhaling. If she started modelling lingerie he would have to take a cold shower. The sound of curtain rings drawing across a rail lifted his gaze for a furtive glimpse of what was headed his way.

A *little* too low, she'd said?

The damn thing was practically at her navel.

All but painted onto her body, the black floor-length sleeveless dress plunged downwards from two thick straps on her shoulders. The globes of her spectacular breasts were barely contained, leading his gaze over the valley of her cleavage to the minuscule black band beneath and the tempting strip of skin beyond that.

She placed her hands on her hips and struck a come-and-get-me pose. 'What do you think?'

It was a bit difficult to think anything when all the blood had rushed from his brain to a point in his body that was so painfully hard he had to stifle a groan.

Silently clearing his throat, he forced a response through tight lips. 'It's nice.'

She arched a brow. *'Nice?'*

Tyler frowned as he raised his chin and looked into her eyes. 'What do you want me to say?'

'Anything other than nice, fine or not bad would make a pleasant change.' She took a deep breath that pushed her breasts forwards and loosened Tyler's grip on his sanity. Then she bent forwards, lowered her gaze and wriggled her shoulders from side to side. 'I'm a bit worried I might pop out of it.'

He sat up and ran his palms over his face. 'How much longer do we have to do this?'

Raising her hands Miranda cupped her breasts as she straightened. By the time she looked at him Tyler had his hands in his lap to hide the evidence of what she was doing to him.

'As long as it takes to get what I want…' A decadent smile formed on her lips as she dropped her hands to her sides. She shrugged. 'There's a reason this is the last appointment on the schedule today. They'll stay open late for me if I need them to. They're awfully good about that and I do love to shop.' Turning, she looked over her shoulder and asked, 'How does it look from the back?'

Like endless miles of flawlessly tanned skin he wanted to touch to discover if it was as soft as it looked. He'd start with his hands, then his mouth, would retrace the path they took with his tongue and blow gently on the wet surface to raise goosebumps while he raised her skirt and…

'I was worried about lines so I thought it was best not to wear anything underneath it.'

Tyler swore viciously inside his head. Gritting his teeth together hard enough to crack the enamel, he managed to bite, 'Where exactly are you planning on wearing that?'

'You think it's too much for something public?'

She stepped over to the mirrors lining one wall so he was treated to a front and back view at the same time. 'You're probably right. Somewhere more intimate would be better. Given the right smoky atmosphere and some sultry music...' She closed her eyes and swayed her hips. 'Mmm...' Her palms followed the curve of her sides from waist to hip. Then she stilled and popped open her eyes. 'I might get this one.'

When she went back into the dressing room Tyler looked at the ceiling and silently asked what he'd done to deserve her. Didn't he have enough to deal with already? He might have miraculously managed to temporarily put his problems to the back of his mind, but it didn't mean they'd gone away. He supposed he should be thankful she hadn't made another escape attempt. But while she was making him suffer for not telling her what had happened outside the school he didn't consider it much of a silver lining.

The door to his left opened and the personal shopper who'd already rolled a rack of clothes into the changing area appeared with another one.

'How is she getting on?' she enquired with a smile as she wheeled it in.

'*Slowly.*'

His response earned a chuckle of laughter. 'You

can't become a fashion icon in this city without putting in long hours of preparation.'

Since he didn't know anything about fashion Tyler would have to take her word for that.

'Is that Janice with the next rack?' a voice called from behind the curtain.

'Yes, I have it here,' Janice replied. 'Is it safe to come in?'

'Absolutely. If you hadn't come back I was going to have to ask Tyler to zip me up.'

While they chatted behind the curtain he pushed to his feet and began pacing the room. After the third lap—and with no new outfit to send him over the edge—he reached into his pocket for his cell phone and called his partner.

'I'm officially in hell,' he said in a low voice.

'The mayor's little girl proving too much of a handful for you?'

'She's *shopping.*'

'I feel your pain, brother.'

'Could you feel it without sounding so amused?' He walked to the other side of the room and glanced at the curtain. 'Give me some good news about the case and I won't hit you the next time I see you.'

While his partner brought him up to speed he made the mistake of turning his back to the changing room. It was only when he ended the call he realized it had gone quiet.

Immediately crossing the room, he threw caution to the wind and yanked back the curtain.

'Son-of-a—'

CHAPTER TEN

'How pissed do you think he'll be when he tracks you down?'

Miranda shrugged as they relaxed in comfortable chairs in the elegant surroundings of the iconic Waldorf Astoria. 'Don't care. He deserves it.'

She didn't mention she'd never met anyone who could irritate the life out of her one minute and make her so hot it felt as if she had a fever in the next. She'd never behaved so provocatively before, purposefully pushing the boundaries of his control to discover how much he could take. It was a perilous game—one she'd thought she had the sense not to play with a man who oozed danger the way Tyler did—but had that stopped her? *Oh, no.*

'You don't feel the least little bit guilty he might get in trouble for losing you?'

'I didn't until you mentioned it so thanks for that—I owe you one.'

Crystal lifted one of the porcelain teacups sitting on the round table between them. 'That conscience of yours has always been a problem. We still need to work on that.'

'You wouldn't have got me this far if I didn't have a natural aptitude for courting trouble.'

'I did say I saw potential in you for greatness when we met.'

'Give me a couple of months to shake off my shackles and I promise to spread my wings and soar,' Miranda vowed.

She heard the clink of the teacup touching a saucer as Crystal took a long breath. 'Nothing to tie you down...no one to get in your way...' She hummed as she exhaled. 'Put all that freedom together with the absence of a guilty conscience and I might have to abdicate my notoriety throne in favour of a worthy successor.'

Drumming her fingers on the arms of her chair, Miranda gently swayed her crossed leg while she tried to convince herself she wasn't watching the foyer for Tyler's arrival. If the stupid man could make up his mind what he wanted it would make things a lot easier.

The way he had looked at her set her body alight, her pulse hammering and her breasts aching for attention. If she had any sense she would have toned it down a little. But the more of a reaction she got from him, the hotter he made her feel, and the desire to push him to breaking point grew. She hadn't been able to stop.

She'd *wanted* him to snap.

If the first time she'd encouraged him with a smile had felt like playing with fire, using her sexuality to get to him was about to turn her into a pyromaniac.

She still didn't like him. She was still mad at him for making her feel like a fool because she'd looked for something that obviously wasn't there. But apparently the thought of angry sex with him did it for her, *big time.*

'You still confident in your fifty-dollar bet on him finding you inside a couple of hours?' Crystal asked.

'If he was as smart as he likes to think he is he would have found me already.'

'If he was as smart as you *say* he thinks he is he would have found Jimmy Hoffa by now.'

She turned her head and smiled ruefully at her best friend. 'So much for my great plan... It doesn't take away from the victory of escaping when he was so determined it wasn't possible. But slinking back to the mansion to find him waiting for me like another disgruntled parent takes the shine off it a little.'

Crystal's gaze moved. 'Well you better dig out your sunglasses because if that's who I think it is headed our way the day just got a whole lot brighter.'

Miranda's gaze immediately shifted to the foyer. The sight of him did its usual snatch and grab with her breath. When his gaze sliced through the air and slammed into hers a heady frisson of excitement travelled through her body. He wasn't just mad. He looked as if he was ready to explode.

'Wow.' Crystal sighed dreamily. 'I want to be in as much trouble as you are right now. Do you think he'll spank you? He looks like he's gonna spank you *good.'*

Her reaction to the suggestion shocked Miranda.

She really was a *very* bad girl.

Exhaling the breath she'd been holding, she smiled sweetly as he marched straight up to them. 'I don't believe you've been formally introduced. Detective Brannigan, meet Crystal—Crystal, meet Tyler.'

'Well, *hello, Tyler.* Is that a gun in your pocket or are you just pleased to meet me?'

A low burst of laughter bubbled up from Miranda's chest when he pressed his mouth into a thin line. 'He doesn't have a sense of humour but I thought it was funny.'

'Awesome,' Crystal replied.

His dark gaze remained firmly fixed on the cause of his anger. 'You're leaving now.'

'Excellent timing. I've just finished my tea. If you hadn't got here I would have had to hail another cab.' She lifted her brows. 'Did you park nearby? I can wait for you to bring the car around front.'

Rage rolled off his large body in waves. 'I'll carry you out of here if I have to.'

'How about we save that for next time?' She reached to the side for her bag and unfolded her legs.

As she got to her feet Crystal held up a set of neatly folded bills. 'The fifty dollars I owe you.'

Miranda turned towards her and flashed a grin, 'Why, *thank you.* It's been a pleasure doing business with you.'

'Any time. Don't forget about that thing at the place we talked about. It should be a blast.'

'I'll see you there.'

'No, she won't,' a deep voice said firmly.

Miranda waved a dismissive hand in his direction. 'Don't listen to him. I never do. Love you.'

'Love you, too.'

Taking the lead, she walked across the foyer with her head held high. When they got to the revolving doors she stopped and angled her chin. 'Oh, dear, this is a bit of a dilemma.' She looked up at him. 'Do you gamble on me going first or risk turning your back on me again? It must be a little like playing roulette for you.'

'Having fun?' he asked through gritted teeth as he captured her elbow in a potentially bruising grasp and bundled them both into a narrow compartment.

'I was till you got here.' But actually, while crushed so tightly against him, she still kinda was.

Wriggling experimentally, she smiled when he tensed.

'You're a piece of work.'

She tugged her elbow free when they hit the sidewalk and he'd pushed her in the right direction. 'You're just upset I slipped through your iron curtain of security. Through a velvet one, no less.'

'Did it ever occur to you if you can find a way out someone can use the same way to get to you?'

'Why would anyone want to get to me?'

'Famous brings out the crazy. I don't even care that you're famous and right this minute *I* want to kill you.'

'How did you find me?' she enquired as they

walked to wherever they were going. She hoped it was far away. She was having entirely too much fun to stop now.

'Your friend Crystal needs to turn off the location option on her Facebook page. And while we're on the subject of the internet any Twittering you do about the places you're going should be done *after* you've been there.'

'They're called Tweets.'

'They're a waving flag that says "come get me, I'm over here."' As they stopped at a crossing he flicked a glare at her. 'Every whack job in the five boroughs could have been waiting for you outside that school.'

'Is that what spooked you?'

'I wasn't *spooked*.' His reaction to the word was so vicious the second time around it gave Miranda the distinct impression she'd hit a nerve. He took a long breath and frowned at how long it was taking for the light to change. 'Someone in the crowd was off.'

Miranda's eyes narrowed. 'Define *"off."*'

'Acting odd—hinky—out of place—obsessively watching your every move.' He captured her elbow again and pushed her across the street.

'You spend all day watching my every move.'

'I'm paid to do it and, believe me, it wasn't my idea.'

'Whose idea was it?' She tugged her elbow. 'You can let go of me now.'

'Not a chance.' He navigated their way through the human traffic on the sidewalk. 'Your head of security used to be my captain's partner back in the day. When he mentioned he needed an injection of new blood it was my misfortune to be volunteered as the wild card.'

Ah-h-h, so *that* was what he meant when he said he'd been trying to get out of it for a week. Considering it was the longest conversation they'd ever had, Miranda thought she should make him angry more often. 'You must have done the close-protection course.'

'Stop changing the subject.'

She sighed heavily as they rounded a corner. 'I think you're overreacting a tad to my having tea at the Waldorf, don't you? Was I dancing on a table when you got there?'

Tyler stopped so suddenly he had to yank her back into place when she got a couple of steps ahead.

'Whoopsies.' Miranda giggled when she almost tripped over, tipsy on the headiness of her success.

He let go of her elbow when she was steady on her feet. 'You don't get it, do you?'

'That this is strike two?' She rolled her eyes. 'I heard you. One more strike and—'

His body loomed over her, the tip of his nose barely an inch away from hers as his voice rumbled, 'Get in the damn car.'

Miranda hadn't even noticed it was there and, frankly, with his mouth in kissing distance, she couldn't care less. She angled her head in a move that suggested she was about to fit their lips together and lifted her chin, reducing the gap to millimetres. Then she looked deep into cobalt-blue eyes and whispered, 'Make. Me.'

The gaze glittering with promise of the danger she so desperately craved wandered lazily over her face. His warm breath mingled with hers while her heart thundered so loudly she could hear it in her ears. It didn't matter that they were standing in the middle of a street in Manhattan. It didn't matter that there were people everywhere and dozens of cars driving by and that pretty much everyone in the universe had a camera on their phone. All that mattered was how badly she wanted to be kissed.

There was nothing beyond burning need and him.

When her heavy-lidded gaze lowered to his mouth she saw a corner of it tug upwards.

'You don't want to do that,' he said in a low, husky, unbelievably sexy voice before moving his head so he could whisper in her ear. 'I'm more trouble than you can handle.'

It was as if he'd placed all of her fantasies within her grasp. Endless possibilities spun around and around in her head in ever decreasing circles with Tyler as the focal point. Miranda blinked at him while he leaned away from her and reached for the door. She turned towards the vehicle and blindly took a step forwards when a thought finally made it through her dizziness. They were just two small words but the weight of their importance felt immense.

'We'll see…'

The voice that said them wasn't hers; it was the sultry voice of the siren she'd always suspected lived somewhere deep inside but had been afraid to seek out. Now she realized the temptress had been with her each time she stepped out of the changing room, had fed on his reaction and was gaining the strength she needed to break free.

As Miranda got into the SUV and he slammed the door shut she experienced the crippling fear that stemmed from the threat of its imminent release.

She didn't know what scared her more: having the siren's call answered by someone she would drag to disaster or having it ignored and remaining isolated and alone, endlessly calling out to someone who would sail through her life without stopping to take a second look.

CHAPTER ELEVEN

IT TOOK intense concentration for Tyler to focus through a blinding rage so he could drive them back to the mansion.

Discovering she'd slipped out through a hidden door in a mural-covered wall at the back of the changing room meant he didn't have to suffer the humiliation of knowing she'd tiptoed out behind his back. But the thought someone might have taken her made him experience his second wave of unwarranted panic in a handful of hours. The realization she'd stood *in front* of the hidden door while he checked the space both eased his mind and made him angry as hell.

The latter feeling grew when he had another moment of clarity. He'd been played since the moment they got there.

By the time he'd searched the store, tracked down Janice and interrogated her until she confessed Miranda had left in a cab there wasn't a rock in the state of New York he wouldn't have turned over to find her. The mayor's head of security would rue the day he'd given him the scope to *'do whatever he needed to do'* when he locked her in a cell and lost the key. His next move was an attempt to get the cab number off the store's security cameras. When that had failed he'd gone hunting for her partner in crime.

Throughout it all he was battling emotions he'd been unable to control since he'd let them out of the damn box. By challenging him to make a move she'd got a glimpse of him few people on the right side of the law ever saw.

That Tyler came from the dark side. He was the man who had spent so long among the dregs of humanity no amount of scrubbing would ever make him clean. He was the lean and hungry one, the cold one, the one who would devour her until he'd taken all she had to give and left her feeling as empty as he did.

She didn't want to mess with that Tyler.

The silence coming from the back seat was a wise move. She could forget a third strike; there wasn't going to be one. What was more, it was time to play the card he'd been holding close to his chest. If she'd behaved he wouldn't have to use it. Now he didn't have a choice.

When they landed back at the mansion he followed her inside and headed straight for the control room. Yanking open one of the drawers on a filing cabinet, he searched for the file he needed and checked the contents. Then he headed for the stairs, taking them two at a time to speed up the process until he reached the hall and marched to her door.

The three sharp knocks he made on the wood were answered with an invitation to come in.

She frowned when he stepped over the threshold and closed the door behind him. 'You can't come in here.'

'You told me to come in.'

'I thought you were *Grace*.'

Holding up the file, he stepped across to the small seating area on one side of the room, pointedly ignoring the presence of her large bed. 'Little light reading for you…' Slapping it down on one of the small tables beside a deeply cushioned armchair, he folded his arms and widened his stance to claim the ground he was standing on. 'I'll wait for questions.'

'You can't *be* here,' she argued as she moved away from the windows. 'What if someone finds you?'

'So long as you don't start another fashion parade we should be fine.'

She scowled at him as she stepped over to pick up the file. 'What is this?'

While she opened the cover and bowed her head to look at the contents he studied her reaction through hooded eyes. Her gaze lifted and sought his before she sat down on the chair farthest away from him. Laying the file on her lap, she turned to the next page.

When she spoke her voice was lower and surprisingly calm. 'How many of these are there?'

'They're the ones we take a closer look at.'

'Because you consider them a potential threat?'

'It's the tone as much as the content. After they're fingerprinted and tested for DNA, a psychologist looks them over and builds a profile.' He shrugged. 'Vast majority of them are sent by fruitcakes still living in the basement of their parents' house when they're forty.'

She flicked a brief glance his way. 'Is that true or are you just saying it to make me feel better?'

'I'd be willing to bet your picture is pinned to more than one of those walls in this city.'

'*Eww.*' She grimaced.

He didn't mention there'd be less of them if people got to know her the way he had in the last forty-eight hours. When he questioned why he hadn't mentioned it, Tyler realized his rage had dissipated. Claiming back a little control probably had something to do with it. Added to the fact they were discussing something that felt closer to police work than babysitting, it was understandable he felt more at ease.

When he noticed the almost imperceptible tremor in her hand as she turned another page Tyler assumed she'd got to one of the more twisted letters.

'Why have I never been shown this file before?'

'They probably thought it was better you didn't know.'

'You obviously disagree.'

As her gaze flickered towards him again the hint of vulnerability he could see in her eyes made him question if he'd done the right thing. He took a short breath. 'Figured if you knew what was out there it might help you understand why things have to change around here.'

'So why not show it to me on the first day?'

Determined he could control her without it would have been the honest answer. But since showing it to her would then be somewhat akin to admitting defeat…

'Wasn't time,' he lied.

She turned her head a little, her gaze searching the air while she gathered her thoughts. As something occurred to her there was a blink of long lashes and she looked him in the eyes again. 'You think the person you saw in the crowd this morning might have sent one of these letters?'

Tyler nodded. 'It's possible. I'll know if I see him again. I'm good with faces.'

She frowned for a moment before confessing, 'I can't believe there are people out there who would write these letters to me. Let alone *mail them*.'

'I told you, famous brings out the crazy.'

'I don't know how I'm supposed to react to this.'

'Calm is good. A lot of folks would be nailing boards over the windows and bulk buying pepper spray by now.'

The comment earned a brief if somewhat half-hearted attempt at a smile before she closed the file and stood up. One of her hands rubbed her hip while she stretched out the other. 'Can you take this with you?' She avoided his gaze. 'I don't want it in here.'

For the first time since he'd entered the room Tyler took a look at his surroundings and realized his mistake. He'd done more than introduce her to the darkness in the world beyond the walls of her cushioned existence—he'd brought some of the sickness he dealt with every day into her haven. But it didn't stop there—one mistake leading directly to another—not only shouldn't he have come to her bedroom, he shouldn't have taken a look around.

It revealed more about her than he'd wanted to know.

Large, bright flowers covered the wallpaper, crystal chandeliers and mirrored glass sparkling in the autumn sunshine pouring through the windows. The furnishings were soft and textured, reminding him what she'd said to a little girl about liking the way things felt.

The penny dropped. She was *tactile*.

It was why she touched so many arms and ruffled heads of tousled hair. She'd demonstrated the same thing when she traced the pearls around her neck. It was part of her inherent sensuality; as witnessed when he'd watched her cup her breasts and smooth her palms over the curves of her body. With the revelation came a question: How did she deal with being surrounded by people who weren't allowed to make physical contact? The need to touch and be touched had to make her as much of a ticking time bomb as him.

It explained a lot when it came to *that kiss*.

The file nodded in front of him, her brows lifting.

Unfolding his arms, he stepped forwards and

took it from her. As he walked back to the door she followed him.

'Tyler?'

He turned to look at her. 'Yeah?'

'Thank you. You're the first person who thought I could handle this and I appreciate that.'

In fairness he hadn't stopped to consider that any more than he'd thought about the repercussions of charging into her bedroom like the proverbial bull in a china shop. But the knowledge softened his stance a little. 'Does it make more sense as to why I've been so rough on you?'

The question garnered a better attempt at a smile. 'It's not just because you're mean and moody?'

'And mysterious, let's not forget that one.'

The knowing gleam in her eyes placed him about two seconds away from offering to touch and be touched, any time she felt the need. If he didn't think she would come out the other side of it a lot worse off than him, he wouldn't have any qualms about being used that way. He doubted any guy who'd watched her dance would. Though he'd never felt the urge to step on a dance floor, he knew what it meant when a woman moved the way she did.

The sexy rotation of her hips, the back-and-forth

movement of her pelvis, the fluid curve of her spine, mile after mile of flawlessly tanned skin with spectacular breasts and long tresses of flame-red hair tumbling over her shoulders and down her back.

Suddenly Tyler could see such a vivid image of her naked he could practically feel her weight on top of him as she hovered on the edge of release.

Time to go.

'I'll see you tomorrow.'

She nodded in reply.

Despite frowning on the way back to the control room he decided—as risky as it was—he would have to pay more attention. He'd missed a lot of clues that had been right in front of his face and that wasn't like him. Prejudice could cloud the evidence, he *knew that*. But now he knew he didn't have all the answers—he had to take a closer look.

If they could find a way to get along better after the tentative truce they'd struck in her bedroom, maybe things would get better and he could focus on something other than sex with a woman who was out of bounds.

Doubtful, but worth a try.

CHAPTER TWELVE

MIRANDA was determined not to let it get to her.

By thinking about the contents of the letters she was allowing whoever had written them to occupy a place inside her head. She refused to give them that but to deny she was rattled would have been pointless. In the following busy days the only time she felt secure was with Tyler around, which was a tad ironic considering the danger *he* posed.

She glanced at him as he completed a check of the room and stopped to run his gaze over the buffet table. 'I'd eat something if I were you. There's not a lot of time for snacks during the speeches stage of the campaign. I think I saw mini-doughnuts somewhere. They're a cop thing, right?'

'Not if the cop wants to stay in shape.'

'You have trouble with your weight?'

'Not everyone is blessed with my godlike physique.'

Miranda stifled a smile as she looked away. It hadn't escaped her attention he'd been working

on his sense of humour lately, even if it demonstrated a distinct lack of anything missing in the
ego department.

Lifting her bag from the floor beside her chair,
she rooted around for the objects she'd brought
with her to help pass the time. Her mother liked to
sit out front in the audience and listen to the never-
ending soliloquies—her daughter, not so much.
Since her father was speaking to a pro-Kravitz
crowd she didn't see the need to be there until they
had to provide a united family front for the press.

With the sheet of paper carefully smoothed out
on the table, she reached for the small box sitting
beside it as Tyler pulled out a chair and joined her.

'What are you doing?'

'I promised I'd finish it.'

'She won't know if you don't.'

'That's not the point.' Miranda shrugged a
shoulder as she selected a slim crayon. 'It's a
karma thing.'

'Careful with those lines.'

'Studying me for a test, Detective, or is everything I say and do so memorable you can't get it
out of your mind?'

'Been working long on that confidence problem?'

She lifted her chin and raised a brow. 'You're

asking me that after the godlike physique comment?'

'That's just stating a fact. You can't argue them.' He selected what looked like a small samosa from the teetering pile on his plate. 'Whereas what you just did? More like wishful thinking.'

When he popped the morsel in his mouth and smirked, Miranda rolled her eyes and continued colouring.

'It's easy to be confident when everything you want gets handed to you,' he said a couple of minutes later.

'I take it we're talking about me again.' She swapped one crayon for another. 'Were you this judgmental with the last person you bodyguarded?'

'I don't think bodyguarded is a word.'

'Is now...'

When she glanced upwards he had his gaze on the open door as an announcement sounded from the auditorium and there was a wave of applause. As he lifted long arms out to his sides in a leisurely stretch the edges of his navy jacket parted, feeding her hungry gaze with the sight of a pale blue shirt stretched taut over his sculpted chest.

Godlike might have been an exaggeration but there was no arguing the man was ripped.

She wondered when he found time to work out and then pictured him hot and sweaty, pumping weights...

'This is my first gig as a bodyguard,' he confessed as he lowered his arms.

Miranda averted her gaze. 'Well, that explains a lot. What did you do before you got here?'

'Police work.'

'What do you call this?'

'Babysitting.'

'I walked right into that one, didn't I?'

'Yup.'

When she glanced upwards again and saw him press his lips together her eyes narrowed. 'Was that a smile?'

'Those little triangle things are spicy.' He tapped a closed fist against his chest. 'Probably indigestion.'

Miranda felt her mouth curve into a smile of her own.

Shifting his weight on the chair, he reached into the inside pocket of his jacket and produced a cell phone, frowning down at the screen as it flashed.

'Are you going to answer that?' she asked.

'It'll wait.'

'Player.'

He looked into her eyes. 'What makes you so sure it's a woman?'

'Isn't it?' She blinked innocently. 'For all I know it could be your wife.'

'How long you been waiting to ask that question?' When she didn't reply he rested his left elbow on the table and showed her the back of his hand. 'Do you see a ring?'

'That doesn't mean anything.'

He lowered the hand to lift something else off his plate. 'Does to me.'

Miranda liked that it did. Without saying so in as many words he'd conveyed he was the faithful type. She didn't have any proof of that without taking his word for it but she knew instinctively it was true. After all, she'd met more than her fair share of liars over the years.

People who attempted to befriend her because of what rather than who she was—who thought they could get her to speak on their behalf to her father or that dating her would deliver their five minutes of fame. She'd met them all and knew she had trust issues as a result.

She would never have the same problems with Tyler. He didn't have an agenda other than doing his job.

Knowing that should have made her feel better but, oddly enough, it didn't.

When she returned her attention to what she was doing, he took a short breath. 'Since we're playing the sharing game, how come it took you so long to have that talk with your mother?'

'Congratulations,' Miranda said dryly. 'It took you a whole four days to bring up the subject. I didn't think you'd last that long.'

'Deflection—I invented that.'

She sighed heavily. 'Mothers and daughters often have complicated relationships.'

'My sister gets on fine with our mom now she's got better about calling her.'

The comment lifted her gaze. 'You have a sister?'

'And three brothers.'

'There are three more of you out there?' The thought was a tad too much for her brain to contemplate.

A corner of his mouth lifted and for the first time—while looking directly at him as it happened—she realized the move lowered the other side. It was almost a yin and yang thing, hinting at two sides of his personality.

'There's only one of me,' he said as if denying the thought she hadn't voiced. 'The rest of them get to spend their time trying to reach the high bar I set for them.'

'You're the eldest?'

'I'm in the middle.'

'I might need you to explain to me how the high bar works if there were two born before you.'

'I raised it,' he replied without skipping a beat. Miranda nodded. 'You tell them that, don't you?'

'Repeatedly.'

She tried to imagine what it must have been like to be part of such a large family. Apart from the freedom they had growing up, she envied the company they would have provided for one another. It made her realize how much she missed having Richie around. He'd be joining the campaign soon and they would have to find the time to talk. She just hoped he could forgive her for breaking their pact.

Pushing the thought from her mind, she jumped into the opening Tyler had given her to get to know him better. 'What do your siblings do?'

'My sister runs the legal department at her husband's company. The rest of us are cops.'

Her gaze lifted again. '*All* of your brothers are with the NYPD?'

'Third generation,' he said with an obvious note of pride. 'It's in the blood.'

'You never wanted to be anything else?'

'Nope.'

It explained where some of his confidence came from. He'd known exactly what he wanted, worked towards it and achieved his goal, whereas Miranda's confidence was born of a need to survive. It wasn't that she didn't have it *now,* but in her teens it was a different story.

'What do you want to be when you grow up?' he asked.

Ouch. But considering she probably deserved it after the way she'd been with him, Miranda let it slide. Instead she set down the crayon and pushed her chair back. 'Do you want something to wash down that mountain of food?'

'Avoidance—I invented that one, too.'

'I'm *thirsty* and a bottle of water might help with your indigestion.' She felt his gaze on her as she approached the buffet table.

'You sure you can manage to find it on your own? Don't you usually have someone to do that for you?'

'There are several things I'm perfectly capable of doing on my own.'

'You're just not given much of a chance to do them...'

'No,' she admitted before lifting a bottle of

water from a bowl of ice and turning to look at him. 'You want one of these or not?'

He nodded. 'Go on.'

There was another announcement as she returned to the table, followed by loud cheering as she stopped by his chair and reached out her arm. Long, warm fingers wrapped around hers as she handed the bottle to him, providing a sharp contrast to its icily dewed surface. Miranda drew in a sharp breath in reaction to the heat travelling up her arm and tingling across her chest to her sensitive breasts. Moving downwards, it pooled low in her abdomen, creating an empty throbbing between her thighs.

When her gaze lifted the intensity in his eyes devoured her, leaving her in no doubt he knew the effect his touch had on her body. What she couldn't understand was why he hadn't done something about it. He didn't strike her as a man who would let something as trivial as boundaries stand in his way.

Part of her was disappointed, another frustrated. But he had no way of knowing she was different with him than she'd ever been with anyone else.

As far as he knew she played the tease with every guy she met, safe in the knowledge if they attempted to cross the line she could simply step behind a protective wall of security personnel and add another tick to a battle of the sexes scorecard. He didn't know how tough it was to date in high school with a bodyguard present. He couldn't imagine how long it had taken for her to lose her innocence to someone who wouldn't consider the virginity of the mayor's daughter a significant notch on their belt. He would *never* know how disappointing the experience had been or that even with determination the three other times she'd managed to find enough privacy to have sex with the same guy hadn't been a whole heap better.

In the end it had led to a bitter break-up, which left scars she covered with a veneer of self-assuredness it had taken years to perfect. Appearances could be deceptive.

A police detective should know that.

Slipping her hand free, she turned away and stepped over to her chair, curling her fingers into her palm as if she felt the need to save some of the warmth of his touch for later. While her father began his speech they both twisted the lids off their bottles and took a drink.

'You haven't answered the question,' he said.

Miranda resisted the urge to look at him. 'Because I know what you're doing. You think by sharing things about your life with me, I'll confide in you.'

'Afraid I'll sell the inside story to the press?'

'No,' she answered honestly. 'Just suspicious about your motives.'

'Cops ask questions. It's what we do,' he reasoned before adding, 'isn't sharing stuff and getting them to empathize how you usually persuade your bodyguards to cut you some slack?'

'I think we've already established I have to work harder than that with you.'

'Which is part of the attraction, isn't it?'

Miranda's gaze snapped up. They were actually going there? Before she made a fool of herself again she had to be sure. 'Attraction?'

The cobalt gaze locked to hers remained steady. 'I think you know what I'm talking about.'

'Maybe you should elaborate.'

'How explicit do you want me to be?'

Miranda ran the tip of her tongue over her lips and watched as his gaze lowered for long enough to follow the movement. 'You think I can't handle explicit?'

If he knew the number of times she'd imagined him telling her exactly what he was going to do to her…

'I think you still don't know you're swimming

out of your depth.' His tone was suddenly hollow and cold.

Subliminally Miranda responded to the accompanying emptiness she thought she could see behind his eyes with the need to offer comfort and return some of the heat he'd created inside her.

She wanted to be alone with him, *really* alone. She wanted him to want the same thing; to ask questions because he wanted to get to know her better and not because he was gathering information to make his job easier.

'Miranda—five minutes.'

The sound of another voice drew her gaze to the open door. 'Thanks, Roger.'

As he disappeared she gathered her things together and placed them back in her bag without looking at Tyler. Reaching inside, she produced the prerequisite Vote Kravitz badge and pinned it to the front of her blouse. 'You want one of these? I always carry a few spares.'

'I didn't vote for him last time.'

Miranda smiled. 'You probably don't want to mention that in front of him. Unless you *want* to hear the one-on-one version of the campaign speech?'

'Any other tips you want to pass on?'

'If he says he'll take it under advisement it means he's going to ignore what you said.'

'Good to know.'

While he cleared the table and walked to the trash can beside the buffet table she checked her appearance in the mirror of a compact and fluffed her hair into place. They met at the door, Tyler waiting silently by her side as she paused to take a breath and fortify herself for the trials ahead. It was time to put on her game face but before she did she allowed him a rare glimpse of a well-kept secret.

As the chill ran down her spine instead of hiding it she shook it off with a shudder of her shoulders. Once she realized what she'd done she glanced sideways and attempted to cover up her vulnerability with a wink. *'Showtime.'*

The low huff of amusement seemed to catch him as off guard as it did her, the immediate following need to shift his gaze to the people assembled behind the stage making Miranda's chest expand with what felt a little too close to endearment. She knew he didn't smile much but suddenly she ached with the need to experience it, to see how it changed his face and hear the sound of rumbling male laughter.

'Your mother is making her way up from the

audience now,' Roger's voice said, encouraging her to step forwards and focus.

When she got a brief glimpse of the packed auditorium as her mother appeared through the curtain at the side of the stage Miranda experienced a flutter of nerves. In need of reassurance, she glanced over her shoulder at Tyler and as their gazes met she thought she could feel it again: the silent understanding she'd been wrong about before.

The nod he gave her was almost imperceptible.

I'm right here, the unexpected warmth in his eyes said. *I've got you.*

She flashed a small smile in reply and for the first time in longer than she cared to admit she didn't feel so alone. It was nice to think someone was there just for her.

Any concern she felt about the truth in the second part of his silent message she could examine later.

CHAPTER THIRTEEN

HE'D been right about one thing.

Miranda was one hell of an actress.

No one on the outside saw how much effort she put into hiding her emotions. Burying them didn't come naturally to her the way it used to for him. But when it came to the way she looked at him— as if he were some kind of tasty treat she wanted to savour—she needed to knock it off. Add their undeniable sexual chemistry to the flash of vulnerability he saw in her eyes before she faced the public and the draw he felt to her was so overpowering Tyler had to remind himself they weren't alone.

He'd have to be careful when they were. The closer she dragged him to the edge, the more likely he was to lose what was left of his footing.

The next time she glanced his way he pointed at the curtain to let her know he would be out front. She nodded in reply before arching a brow at her mother when the woman reached out to brush her hair away from the badge she'd pinned to her chest.

'Seriously?'

'I'm not permitted to make motherly gestures now?'

'Not if it takes us back to the days when you used to dress me like a Jackie Kennedy doll.'

Content she had something to distract her from any fear she felt of unseen dangers in the auditorium, Tyler moved into position. Standing where he had one-hundred-and-eighty-degrees' coverage from the front of the stage, he checked everyone else on the combined detail was where they were supposed to be before running his gaze over the crowd.

'...and with your help we can finish what we started...'

As the mayor's speech whipped the crowd into a frenzy the cheers became louder, making it difficult for Tyler to hear if anything came through in his earpiece. The ever-present tension in his body coiled tighter as he raised his hand and used his forefinger to push it tighter into place.

'We've come too far to give up now!' the mayor shouted into the microphone. 'Are you with me?'

The crowd yelled, 'Yes!'

'Are you with me?'

'Yes!'

There were too many banners and placards waving wildly in the air to allow him to check every face. It made Tyler antsy, the fingers of his gun hand flexing at his side.

'Then let's *do it!'*

'Kravitz! Kravitz! Kravitz! Kravitz!'

In the midst of the chanting there was what sounded like popping gunfire. Immediately pushing back his jacket to place a thumb on his service weapon, Tyler snapped his gaze in the direction he thought it came from. There wasn't any screaming; the crowd wasn't panicking—somewhere in his mind he knew they were both indications nothing had happened. But while his body created so much adrenaline it made his heart struggle to pump it through his veins his brain ignored the message.

In the end it took the sight of a woman scolding her son as she confiscated a bunch of balloons for him to avoid calling in the threat and drawing his weapon.

Lowering his arm, he ground his teeth together, self-recrimination searing his throat when he glanced at the stage. Miranda was standing in plain sight, smiling and waving with her parents.

As her gaze sought him out the need to go to her and haul her into his arms was crippling.

He didn't want her up there. He wanted her somewhere he knew she was safe. The thing that stopped him from jumping onstage and carrying her away wasn't his job or who her father was; it was the certainty that place of safety wasn't with him.

By the time they were driving back to the mansion through a not-so-safe-after-dark neighbourhood he was strung out and close to breaking point.

'You okay?'

'Yes,' he gritted. But it was a lie. If he didn't find an outlet for some of his tension soon...

When a figure walking down the sidewalk caught his eye Tyler's brain ran through a scrolling roll of faces and hit jackpot. Checking for traffic, he turned the wheel and swung the Escalade around.

'Where are we going?' she asked.

He didn't reply as the figure turned a corner. Instead he followed it, drew to a halt and unbuckled his seat belt. 'Lock the doors and stay inside.'

'What are you—?'

'Keys are in the ignition.' He got out and slammed the door. As the man lit up by the headlights turned and looked over his shoulder he called out, 'Hey, Jimmy, remember me?'

The second he rabbited Tyler gave chase. One wrong turn later the idiot was trapped in a dead-end alley.

'Haven't you learnt you can't run from me?' He slammed him face-first into a wall before patting him down. 'Out doing a little business—what do we have here?' He took a step back and looked down at the clear plastic pouch in his hand. 'Looks like I have you on possession…'

'That's not mine. It belongs to a friend.'

'Do I look like I just got hit by the stupid stick?'

When the idiot made a predictable attempt to escape it was all the incentive Tyler needed to cut his dark side loose. Reaching for a wrist, he twisted the arm, spun him around and slammed him back into the wall. When he leaned closer his voice was purposefully menacing.

'You know what I want.'

'I heard you was off the case.'

'You heard wrong.'

'You can't rough me up. I'll file a complaint.'

'Go ahead,' Tyler told him as he twisted the arm hard enough to dislocate a shoulder and used his other hand on the guy's head to press his cheek to the wall. 'In the meantime here's what's gonna

happen. You're gonna take a message to Demietrov for me. I'll keep the sentences nice and
short so you can remember them. You tell him
I'm coming for him. He won't know where. He
won't know when. Tell him to keep looking over
his shoulder.'

'You're Dirty Harry now?'

'No.' His mouth curled into a threatening smile.
'I'm his worst nightmare. You don't deliver the
message I'll be yours, too. I'll spread the word
you're my new best friend.' He felt his hand press
harder against the man's skull and ignored the cry
of pain while he fought the need to crush bone.
'No witnesses here. It'll be your word against
mine and I think we both know you're the weak-
est link.'

'She's a witness,' Jimmy croaked.

CHAPTER FOURTEEN

MIRANDA'S breath caught when Tyler's gaze snapped towards her. Fear trickled down her spine, creating goosebumps on her skin and chilling her bones. The violent edge to the scene, the savage need for blood pervading the air—they were valid reasons to fear the man she barely recognized.

Somewhere deep in her soul she could hear a voice calling out to him, 'What are you doing? This isn't *you.*'

But how could she know that for sure?

He released his captive. *'Go.'*

As the man ran towards her Miranda took an instinctive step back. By the time she looked at Tyler again she could sense the hostility aimed at her. Tendrils of rage flowed through the air with the oppressive weight of a brewing storm. 'I told you to stay in the car with the doors locked. What part of that didn't you understand?'

'I…uh…' She cleared her throat and tried to find her voice. 'I was never that good at taking orders.'

'I suggest you start.' He stepped forwards and past her, his muscles carrying him with the same fluidity of movement she would have associated with a panther.

Her first impression of him as a predator crouched to spring on its prey had been right. She just hadn't realized how lethal he could be until she saw him in action.

She hesitated before following him, torn between the need to know what had happened and an almost childlike desire to hide. Her gaze darted to the shadows between overflowing Dumpsters, her imagination filling them with everything from rats to Freddie Krueger.

Better the devil—even if it was plainly obvious she didn't know him that well.

'Tyler.' She had to run to catch up. 'Tyler, *wait.*'

He stopped so abruptly she almost tripped face-first into his back.

'That's the second time you've done that.' She frowned at his chest when he turned around. 'A little warning would be good.'

Chancing an upwards glance at his shadowed face she discovered he was looking at her through dark hooded eyes.

'What just happened?'

'Did you lock the Escalade?'

'Yes.'

'Where are the keys?'

She reached into the scooped neckline of her blouse to retrieve them from her bra, jangled them in front of his face and snatched them away before he lifted his arm.

Tyler waggled his fingers at her. 'Hand them over.'

'I don't think so.' She tucked them back into her bra. 'You want them you're going to have to come get them.'

'You think I won't?'

'I think I'll scream at the top of my lungs if you *try.*' As far as she was concerned he wasn't getting them back until he gave her an explanation. She folded her arms over her breasts to protect her bargaining tool. 'I'm assuming that man wasn't a friend of yours.'

'Good guess.' The corner of his mouth lifted in a move resembling a sneer. 'I haven't made many friends on the periphery of the Russian mob recently.'

Miranda's jaw dropped. 'That's a joke, right?' A small burst of nervous laughter left her lips. 'Next thing you'll be saying you like your Martinis shaken, not stirred.'

'I'm not a spy.'

'We've already established you weren't a body-guard until recently. So what are you?'

He shook his head and turned away, glancing at her from the corner of his eye as she unfolded her arms and fell into step beside him. 'I'm a street cop—narcotics. The bodyguard thing is a temporary gig.'

'But you're still working on a case, aren't you?'

'Stopping the flow of drugs in any city with a market for them is like trying to empty the ocean with a teaspoon. I can't afford to take time off.'

'Then why are you babysitting me?'

'I've asked that question several times.'

'But if you've never been a bodyguard?'

'I took the close protection course a few years ago,' he told her as they turned a corner. 'Back in the days when I had a career plan I was gonna spend time in every department and work my way up.'

Naturally she wanted to know what had happened to knock him off course but first things first. 'How long have you been with Narcotics?'

'Three years—transferred from Vice.'

'How long have you been a police officer?'

'Coming up on twelve years.'

She blinked in surprise. He must be older than he looked. 'What age are you?'

'Thirty-two—ask a lot of questions when you're scared, don't you?'

'I'm not scared,' she lied. 'I'm…' Her head nodded a little from side to side as she sought the right words. When none was forthcoming she opted for a smidgeon of truth. 'Okay, I was scared. I've never seen anyone… I mean, not in real life… obviously on TV and in movies but—'

'View's not so great away from the ivory tower, is it?' he said dryly. 'Down here on street level things can get dirty. I know of at least two cold-case homicides in this area in the last couple of years.'

She glared at his tense profile. 'Are you trying to scare me again?'

The question made him stop and turn towards her. 'What you just saw wasn't enough for you?'

Even in the restricted light Miranda could see his gaze burned with anger. Having faced it before—and with the recent addition of visible proof—she realized how much constraint he exercised when she pushed him. What she found more difficult to understand was how he made her feel and how swiftly it returned to the same unwavering constant over and over again.

She was drawn to him—had been from the

start—and even after seeing him at his most dangerous it hadn't changed.

'That didn't look like you,' she replied.

The man she'd seen in the alley wasn't the one who had been watching over her.

'You think you know me after less than a week?' He jerked his brows. 'Is this the part where you tell me danger does it for you—that you're into bad boys and want to be taken on a wild ride?'

Yes, but there was wild and then there was suicidal.

He took an ominous step forwards. 'That's what you were looking for from that dance floor. It's why you responded the way you did when I kissed you. Do you know what happens to women who go looking for trouble? I do. But maybe what you need is a little taste of what you're getting into.'

Miranda's breath snagged in her throat as he took another step forwards, her eyes widening as she took a reciprocal step back. 'Tyler, *don't.*'

'Too late, princess.'

The man obviously had a thing with pinning people to walls because the next thing she knew Miranda had her back to one, the cold dampness of the bricks through the thin material of her blouse making her jump forwards. The move literally played her directly into his hands. Grasping her wrists, he lifted her arms above her head and pushed her back into the wall with his body.

Hard, he was hard everywhere, muscular and tight, his grip on her wrists unyielding as he trapped them in one large hand to free up the other. Miranda struggled against him, the movement merely adding to her problems when her traitorous body responded with a gush of heat to her core. He angled his head, his lips hovering above hers, tempting, teasing, the muscles in his torso so tense they rippled with each harsh breath.

'You think you can stop me now?' When he spoke his mouth whispered across hers. The hand he'd freed smoothed into the dip of her waist on the side of her body before lowering to her hip and squeezing tight enough to make her feel the imprint of each finger. Moving lower, he fisted a handful of skirt material and slowly dragged it upwards. 'Go ahead and try.'

It was pure hell not to give in to temptation and kiss him. If there was trust between them she wouldn't resist; might even have encouraged him not to stop. But no matter how desperately she clung to the belief he wouldn't hurt her, Miranda couldn't deny her desire was woven with a thread of fear. Her heart pounded painfully against her breastbone, her body shaking from the inside out.

He was both stronger and bigger than her—there was no way she could fight him off. She'd never been made so aware of the weakness of her body before.

As the skirt slid higher he forced a leg between her knees and nudged them apart. 'I could take you in this position whether you want me to or not.'

She drew in a ragged breath as she stopped struggling and swore he wouldn't make her cry. 'This isn't you.'

'You don't know that,' he said harshly. 'You could have been sidling up to a monster with that little game of dress up you played. I could have brought you here because I know it's a place where people ignore screams after dark.' His voice lowered. 'I could be inside you right now—taking what I need without caring if you get any pleasure out of it. And when I'm done I could leave your broken body for someone else to find.'

'You wouldn't do that.' The crackle of emotion in her voice was impossible to disguise. Swallowing the sob she didn't want him to hear, she forced her gaze upwards to the fire escape on the wall opposite them, willing her mind to detach from her body so he couldn't touch a part of her that might never heal.

When her vision blurred she blinked rapidly but was unable to stop the tears that spilled over her lower lashes to blaze a heated trail down her cheeks.

'Isn't this what you wanted all along—you and me, together?' he asked in his coarse, cold voice. 'You've been begging for it from the start.'

'Not like this,' she choked.

Whether it was the honesty, the pain in her voice, how badly her body was shaking or that he could taste the tears trickling into her mouth, she didn't know. But suddenly his hand stilled, his fingers loosened and a deathly silence descended. It couldn't have lasted for more than a handful of seconds but felt like an eternity. Then, without warning, he released her and staggered back as if he'd been repelled by an invisible force.

When she looked at him Miranda didn't need better light to see the mixture of fury, self-loathing and guilt on his face; she could feel it swirling in a maelstrom around him. He moved sharply, pacing a restless circle while viciously spitting a litany of self-recrimination that was downright nasty. She winced as she straightened her skirt with shaking hands. The self-hatred was more than obvious and with blinding clarity she got an inkling of what he might have been doing.

It was more than a brutal warning of the consequences her actions could have with the wrong man—it was an attempt to get her to hate him as much as he hated himself.

When he stopped pacing he shook his head. 'You need a new bodyguard. I'm obviously not cut out for this.'

Gathering strength, she took a tentative step forwards and dampened her lips with the tip of her tongue. 'I don't want a new bodyguard. I want you.'

'How can you *say that* after what I just did to you?'

He snarled like a cornered animal but with new insight Miranda saw him as less of a predator and more of an angry bear with a thorn in his paw.

She took another step. 'You wouldn't have hurt me.'

'You don't *know* that!' His mouth twisted when he saw her hesitate. 'You gonna try lying to me and telling me you didn't have a moment of doubt?'

'I can't do that,' she confessed. 'But I can remember the man you were before you turned the car around.'

His chest heaved as he tried to gain control. 'What do I have to do to make you realize you'd be better keeping your distance from me?'

'I don't know. But this wasn't it.'

'I'm not like the other guys you've spent time with. There's nothing polished or refined about me.'

If he was trying to discourage her from reaching out to him, then he wasn't doing a very good job. The compulsion she'd felt to offer comfort combined with her need for physical contact, drawing her to him with a sense of what felt like inevitability. She took another step forwards and another until she was standing directly in front of him.

'Right now I need you to hold me for a minute,' she said softly. 'Do you think you can do that?'

'You should be running for the hills,' he replied in a gruffer voice. 'Not asking me to get closer.'

'I need a little shoulder action.' When she attempted a smile the fear of rejection she'd hidden since her teens made it waver. 'If you can think of anyone else I can ask for that when everyone who surrounds me isn't supposed to touch me—'

He reached out and hauled her into his arms.

Miranda gasped at the contact and let out a small sob of relief. Wrapping her arms around his lean waist, she buried her face in his chest and took several breaths of Tyler scented air. She could feel the tension in his body, streams of electricity buzzing beneath his skin. But she'd been right to ask him to hold her. A violent shudder ran through him, his arms tightening as if he couldn't hold her close enough. After a while he rested his chin on her head and she felt his throat convulse.

'I'm sorry,' he said roughly, the impression it wasn't something he said very often making her heart twist.

'I know.' She turned a little and rested her cheek against his tie. 'It's okay. I forgive you.'

'You shouldn't. I can't forgive me.'

'Maybe you should start.' She took another breath before jumping in with both feet. 'What happened to make you so angry, Tyler?'

'How do you know you didn't just get a glimpse of the real me?'

'Because you're holding me right now and giving me what I need.' She snuggled closer to prove the point before confessing, 'And because I don't want to believe it was…'

When he moved his head she felt the whisper of his breath against her hair. 'You can't save me, if that's what you're thinking. I'm beyond saving.'

Leaning back to look up at his face, she discovered he was frowning; his gaze lowered so she couldn't look into his eyes. The arms holding her loosened as he took a half step back. Unwilling to let him retreat when they'd taken such a major leap forwards, Miranda freed up a hand and raised it to stroke her fingertips along his jaw, her thumb gliding to the edge of his mouth.

Heat resonated from him, seeping into her skin and removing the chill from her bones.

Watching her thumb as it traced his lower lip, she whispered, 'Kiss me.'

He stood rigidly still.

Moving her hand to wrap her fingers around the thick column of his neck, she pulled his head down to hers and rocked forwards onto her toes. She lifted her chin, closed the last of the distance between them and pressed her lips against his. He stiffened but didn't jerk away. Miranda took that as a good sign, even if she'd never kissed such an unresponsive partner. Launching a tentative exploration, she kissed a corner of his mouth, willing him to relax.

The thought of him remaining still while she explored every inch of his body was a heady enticement to continue. Emboldened, she traced the valley between his lips with the tip of her tongue. Then she wasn't in control any more.

Long fingers threaded into her hair, his palm cradling the back of her head and holding it still as he sampled her lips in softly sipping kisses that coaxed her into opening her mouth. When his tongue slipped inside Miranda moaned in appreciation, sensation pouring over her like a blanket of warm honey. Another large hand stroked over her shoulder blade as the kiss deepened, smoothing down her spine and dipping to the curve of her rear to draw her closer.

When her abdomen made contact with the evidence that he was as turned on as she was Miranda grabbed the lapels of his jacket between her fingers. He parted their lips and she dropped her head back, eyes closed, as he planted a trail of heated kisses along her neck. He pushed up the hem of her blouse, burrowing his hands underneath to touch the heated skin of her midriff. When she sucked in a breath the movement granted him access to her torso. He traced a finger along the band of her bra, knuckles skimming the lace-covered swell at the underside of her breasts.

'We shouldn't be doing this,' his deep voice rumbled against her neck.

'I'm not sure reminding us both it's forbidden will help,' she answered breathlessly, clinging to him as if he was the only thing holding her up-right.

'I'm supposed to keep my distance.'

Her mouth curved into a decadent smile. 'That might sound more convincing if you weren't saying it while you have your hands on me.'

'You're the mayor's daughter,' he said as he kissed his way back up her neck.

'One day I'm hopeful people will think of me as more than that. Using my name would be a great place to start.'

He raised his head and looked down at her. 'I've used your name.'

'No, you haven't.'

'I can't have gone this long without saying it.'

She smiled again. 'Wanna bet?'

'There was that time when I was listing everything I knew about you…'

She shook her head. 'Doesn't count.'

He nudged the tip of her nose with his before lowering his voice. 'Miranda…'

The sound of her name said in the deep rumble of his voice sent a tingle across her sensitive skin.

He placed a light kiss on her lips. *'Miranda…'*

She sighed contentedly. It sounded both sexy and reverent when he said it that way. Angling his head, he scrambled her thoughts with a longer, heated kiss. She felt one of his hands move against her breast and then…

He lifted his head and took a step back, his hands dropping from her body.

When Miranda opened her eyes she blinked at the sight of a half smile curving his mouth as he held up the keys.

'Nice move,' she said with begrudging respect.

He clamped his fingers around the keys and lowered his arm. 'I have plenty more where that came from but right now you're going home before we both end up in trouble.'

When he took her hand and led her back to the SUV, her thoughts unscrambled for long enough to allow something she'd overheard in the alley to make its way through to the front of her mind. 'The guy you sent a message to—isn't there a chance he'll come looking for you when he gets it?'

'He won't try anything when I'm on duty.'

'How do you know that?'

'Not his MO. If he has the stones to come after a cop he'll do it in the shadows.' Long fingers flexed around hers. 'Despite evidence to the contrary I wouldn't do anything that could place you in danger.'

'It wasn't me I was worried about.'

The softly spoken words made Tyler stop dead in his tracks and turn towards her. 'I won't let anything happen to you.' His voice was suddenly deeper, richer and accompanied by what almost felt like déjà vu. 'You can trust me.'

The level of intensity seemed out of place, even for him. Miranda searched what she could see of his eyes. 'What aren't you telling me?'

He shook his head. 'Nothing.'

A sense of foreboding created an unfamiliar heaviness in her chest. 'Tyler—'

'I think we've covered enough ground for one night, don't you?'

He had a point. Suddenly she was exhausted in a way she'd never been before, both physically and emotionally. What worried her was how badly she wanted to draw strength from him and how quickly she'd become reliant on him being there. It wasn't like her.

From the night they met she'd been following his lead. Even when she'd resisted she'd been caught in the undertow of a wave of attraction, unable to come up for air. At some point she knew she would have to—he wouldn't be there for ever. But until that day and while there was something that made it feel she should hold on to him, she wrapped a second hand around his and held on tight.

CHAPTER FIFTEEN

'I'M HEARING rumours on the streets there's a rogue cop gunning for Demietrov. Tell me it's not you.'

When Tyler silently took the fifth his partner swore in his ear. 'This isn't the Wild West where you can clean up the streets with a gun. Hang on.' He raised his voice to yell at someone who had obviously walked in on his end of the conversation. 'Anyone wants me I'll be in the porcelain reading room.' His voice lowered again. 'I haven't been keeping you in on the loop so you can turn vigilante on me. You can't take on every low life in the city. What difference do you think one man can make?'

'We think that way we've got no business being cops,' Tyler replied flatly. For him there was more to carrying a shield than family tradition. He'd signed up to make a difference; his lack of success over the years more than half his problem. A little never felt like enough. Textbook overachiever most likely, but the way he saw it there was no point doing something if it wasn't done right.

'Do what you're thinking about doing and you won't be a cop for much longer,' his partner replied. There was the sound of a creaking door being opened. 'You seem to be under the impression 'cos you're not married with kids it means no one will get hurt if something happens to you. How do you think your family would feel about that?'

Probably the same way they'd feel if they'd had ring seats when he'd treated Miranda the way he had. Like all good Irish boys he'd been raised to be respectful to women. Hadn't been much indication of that with her, had there? His mother would tear strips off his worthless hide if she knew what he'd done. But when it came to how his family would feel if he became part of the darkness he'd been fighting for so long, Tyler realized he'd convinced himself they would understand. Be disappointed in him—no doubt about that—but they'd get it. Miranda wouldn't.

Not so long ago what she thought hadn't mattered.

But it did now.

She'd been worried about him. No matter how hard he tried he couldn't wrap his head around that. Being offered forgiveness with soft, sweet kisses he found impossible to resist had been difficult enough for him to understand. But that she'd been *worried about him?*

'You listening to me?'

'I can hear you.'

'Not what I asked.'

Tyler watched the people going about their business with cell phones pressed to their ears, cups of coffee in their hands, briefcases as extensions of their arms or a combination of all the above. New Yorkers living busy lives and never worrying about crime until something happened to them. It was the way it should be but it took a thin blue line of defence to keep it that way.

He wondered when he'd first thought about crossing it and then questioned for the hundredth time why he'd made the exact same vow to Miranda he'd made to the woman who'd died when he couldn't live up to his word.

'Did it occur to you by calling him out he might come gunning for you?' his partner asked. 'What am I saying? Course it did. You think by painting a target on your back you'll force him out of hiding. I thought we had a *plan*.'

'We're barely making a dent in his operation. Every time we take his dealers off the streets he replaces them before we've had time to do the paperwork.'

'What if he puts a price on your head and the mayor's daughter gets caught in the crossfire?'

It was an unnecessary reminder of his thoughtlessness but in his defence it had been a while since he stopped to consider the effect his job could have on someone else. Once he did he realized his need to protect her had nothing to do with duty any more. It was personal. She made him wish the world were a better place, adding to the dissatisfaction he couldn't do more to make it that way.

Placing some distance between them was the only way he could focus clearly.

When she was around it had got to the point where every step he took and every thought he had was centred on the knowledge she was nearby. She clouded his judgment and weakened what was left of his resolve not to sleep with her. He couldn't seem to be near her without wanting to touch her. Wherever possible he found himself offering a hand to help her in or out of a vehicle, placing his palm on the inward curve of her spine to guide her in the right direction, handing bottles of water to her or taking them away when she didn't need them any more.

Her reaction to each stolen touch or heated glance made him forget all the reasons he couldn't have her. But he needed to remember them, for his sake as much as hers.

'…till you give me your word you won't do anything stupid,' his partner's voice said.

Tyler frowned. 'Didn't catch all of that.'

'The hell you didn't.'

He stopped in front of a storefront. 'I gotta go. I'll talk to you later.'

'Don't hang up on—'

Hitting the screen to end the call, he pushed through the door, walked to the nearest member of staff and flashed his shield. 'Detective Brannigan—I noticed the lion on your company logo and was wondering if I can take a look at some of your stationery.'

While the woman led the way he checked his watch. Two hours fourteen minutes and twenty-eight seconds until he saw Miranda again. Not that he was counting.

Under normal circumstances they would be locked on a heading he suspected neither of them wanted to change. But kissing her was one thing, taking advantage of their enforced proximity to scratch an itch was another and all it could be. Apart from keeping her safe and being there when she needed him, he had nothing to offer. There'd been a time he'd thought about settling down, getting married, having kids and moving up the ranks so his family could be proud of him. But even if she wanted a commitment from a guy like him, those days were gone.

His partner's concern wasn't misplaced. One way or another there would be a day of reckoning. It had been a long time coming and when it did Tyler wasn't convinced he would do the right thing.

Standing close to one of the windows he looked outside and saw a silent figure standing on the other side of the street, dull, lifeless eyes staring at him with accusation.

He wondered how Miranda would react if he mentioned he could see dead people.

CHAPTER SIXTEEN

SHE missed him when he wasn't around. That Tyler had become such a strong presence in her daily life concerned Miranda, but not enough to distract her focus from the increased frustration it added to the lack of privacy.

Detective Patty-Fingers was going to drive her insane if she couldn't get him on board with the idea of some quality alone time soon.

Adding the finishing touches to her make-up, she leaned back from the mirror and forced the ever-present thread of worry from her mind. Knowing the work he did allowed her imagination to run riot with dozens of horrific scenarios, all of which resulted in him getting hurt.

That no one would think she needed to know if he was didn't exactly help.

Reaching for an assortment of mismatched gold bangles to accompany the chunky squares dangling from her ears, she stood up, pushed her feet into a pair of waiting Jimmy Choo's and stepped over to the full-length mirror for a final inspection. The fashion police would be out in force on the red carpet but, for the first time since they'd started tearing apart everything she wore, she didn't care what they said. So long as the short shift of cap-sleeved emerald-green material overlaid with fine black lace got Tyler's attention nothing else mattered.

The flutter of tiny wings tickled the inside of her stomach with anticipation as she lifted her purse from the end of the bed and crossed the room. It wasn't a *date* they were going on but it felt like one.

He was effortlessly taking the stairs two at a time when she walked down the hall, his gaze lifting to tangle with hers. As always, her breath caught. Now it really did feel like a date. He wasn't wearing a suit. Instead his long legs were encased in black jeans and he'd layered the top half of his body with a dark sports jacket worn over a V-necked sweater with a white T-shirt underneath.

They met at the top of the stairs, his gaze slowly caressing her from head to toe before he quirked his brows and rewarded her efforts with, 'Wow.'

A smile blossomed on her lips. 'Exactly the response I was aiming for.' She angled her chin. 'Are both your suits at the dry cleaner's?'

'I heard bodyguards were supposed to blend in at these things. And for the record, I have more than two suits.'

'Are they all navy and black?' She resisted the urge to reach out and brush her fingertips over the lapels of his jacket while they were under the scrutiny of the security cameras. 'Now that I think about it, do you even have any colour in your wardrobe?'

To her delight he looked amused. 'You gonna start dressing me now?'

Au contraire; while he looked as mouth-wateringly good as he did, she was much more interested in *undressing* him.

When he read the message in her eyes he shook his head and inclined it towards the stairs. 'Let's go, princess.' They were halfway down before he lowered his voice to ask, 'You're wearing underwear under this one, right?'

'Only one way you're going to find out,' she replied in an equally intimate tone. 'And did I mention this is supposed to be kiss-proof lipstick? We might need to conduct a consumer test later.'

As they stepped onto the foyer the weight of a large hand on the inward curve of her spine drew a sharp breath through her lips. She could feel each long finger, her body aching in all the places she wanted him to touch. Then the door to the vestibule opened, her father appeared and Tyler's hand dropped a split second before he took a noticeable step back.

She hated that he had to do that.

'I thought you were speaking at a dinner this evening,' Miranda said to her father with a smile.

'Came back to get your mother,' her father replied. 'Where are you off to?'

'Movie premiere in Times Square. I'm afraid Detective Brannigan will have to suffer his way through a rom-com.'

Her father leaned in to place a kiss on her cheek. 'Have fun, sweetheart.'

'You, too.'

He nodded at Tyler. 'Detective.'

'Sir.' Tyler nodded in reply.

They continued across the foyer and into the vestibule as her father made his way upstairs. When Miranda used one of the tricks she'd learnt and slowed her pace so Tyler would touch her again the outer door opened and Lou Mitchell walked in.

'Miranda.' He smiled.

'Good evening, Lou. How's the family?'

'Great, thanks.' He looked at Tyler. 'How'd you get on this afternoon?'

'Might have something,' Tyler replied. 'I'll talk to you tomorrow.'

Miranda lowered her voice as they stepped outside. 'This place is like Grand Central.'

'Yeah, I'd noticed that. But at least we'll get some peace and quiet in Times Square.'

The combination of dry humour and the thought he might be as frustrated by the lack of privacy as she was made her smile. 'What were you doing this afternoon?'

'That's on a need-to-know basis.' He stopped at the front of the SUV. 'Where do you think you're going?'

'I want to sit up front.'

He shook his head. 'No.'

'Why not?'

'Have you ever sat in the jump seat?'

'No.'

'Then you're not starting now.' Raising a hand he beckoned her with a crooked forefinger. 'Round you come.'

Miranda stood her ground. 'I thought we were parking at the Hyatt.'

'We are.'

'Then it's not like I'm getting out where anyone can see me, is it?'

'That's not the point.'

'We'll be late if you don't open the door.'

Tyler nodded. 'Best come round here and get in, then, hadn't you?'

She rolled her eyes. 'I can't believe we're arguing about where I sit.'

'And I can't believe you're kicking up such a stink about it when you've never sat anywhere else.'

Miranda aimed a mock glare his way. 'Maybe it might be nice not to feel like I'm being chauffeured everywhere.'

'You *are* being chauffeured everywhere.'

'You could indulge me just this once,' she cajoled.

'Not paid to do that.'

She batted her lashes and pouted, 'Pretty please?'

Tyler sighed heavily before the finger he'd used to beckon her pointed in warning as he moved. 'No touching anything while I'm driving.'

Why did he think she wanted to sit in the front?

'I *mean* it.'

He was still a party pooper but, the way Miranda looked at it, the night was young.

When the locks clicked she opened the door and climbed inside, carefully arranging her dress so it wouldn't crease and then sliding the skirt a little higher so it revealed a couple more inches of leg. As they reached for their seat belts she glanced surreptitiously at Tyler to see if he'd noticed. Judging by the frown on his face as he turned the ignition key, he had.

She wondered if teasing him would ever get old. He had to know it was foreplay. There was nothing about him that suggested he didn't have skills in that area. When she thought about what he could teach her, she squirmed a little on the seat.

'Quit that,' he said in a rougher voice as the gate raised and they left the compound.

'I'm settling in.' She looked out of the windscreen and stifled a smile. 'It feels different sitting up here.'

'That's not what you're doing.' He checked for traffic before turning onto the street.

'Are you an expert on how a woman's mind works?'

He aimed another heated gaze her way. 'I know getting inside a woman's head can have spectacular results in the bedroom, if that's what you're asking.' When he focused on driving again, he

frowned. 'Most cops learn to read body language.
It comes in handy.'

Nice attempt at trying to change the subject.

Miranda turned towards him, much more interested in what was happening inside the SUV
than she was in anything outside. 'How do you
do that?'

'Read body language?'

'Get inside a woman's head.'

'You pay attention.'

'So what have you discovered about me?'

'You're not who I thought you were,' he replied
with a hint of uncharacteristic reluctance. 'Not
entirely.'

She took a deep breath. 'I'm not sure I'm going
to like everything about the answer to this question, but here goes. What do you mean by "not
entirely"?'

'You're high-maintenance.'

Miranda disagreed. 'Unless someone is supply-
ing the necessary personal grooming must-haves
of a mani-pedi or a fabulous haircut I manage my
beauty regime the same way any other woman
does.'

'That wasn't what I meant.' He checked the mirrors before changing lanes. 'You're hard work.'

She could see how that would be true from his

point of view. 'Do I need to remind you that you weren't exactly Mr Friendly at the start? I might have been nicer to you if you'd been nicer to me.'

'You telling me you don't like getting your own way?'

'Most people do,' Miranda countered. 'Especially if it can mean the difference between surviving in an environment you find suffocating or drowning under the weight of a responsibility you never asked for in the first place.'

When she realized how much she'd revealed she fixed her gaze on the traffic in front of them. She couldn't expect him to understand how she felt. No one could until they'd walked a mile in her shoes.

'I already figured that part out,' his voice rumbled.

'It's not as easy a life as some people might think it is,' she confessed.

'I couldn't do it.'

'You wouldn't have let it continue for so long.'

'I'm surprised you have.'

'As crazy as they can make me, I love my family.' She shrugged a shoulder. 'They're the only one I've got.'

With the reminder she lifted her chin and sat taller. Young ladies didn't slouch; they had poise and composure, even when having a discussion that made them feel exposed and vulnerable to criticism.

'You don't have to do that when we're alone. Save it for the crowd.'

Miranda's startled gaze leapt to his profile.

As he straightened the wheel he glanced at her. 'You thought I didn't know?'

It was difficult to think anything when the sensation he really had stepped inside her head was so...*unsettling*...

'Everyone has a front,' he continued while she tried to find her voice. 'Work the streets for long enough you learn there's usually a reason for it.'

Having raised the topic, he had to know she would turn it around. 'What do you hide?'

The corner of his mouth lifted. 'If I answered that question it wouldn't be hidden any more, would it?'

'You've spent more than your fair share of time in an interrogation room, haven't you?'

'They're called interview rooms these days.'

When she wondered how much his job affected the rest of his life Miranda decided the easiest way to find out was to open the topic. 'It can't be easy not to bring your work home with you.'

'It's not.'

'So how do you strike a balance?'

A muscle in his jaw clenched. 'You accept the fact you made a vow and live up to it as best you can for as long as you can.'

She understood that better than he probably thought she did. What she didn't understand was how he dedicated so much of his life to his work without needing something for himself. Didn't he have things he enjoyed doing in his downtime— people he wanted to spend time with, places he wanted to see? She couldn't have survived if she didn't have those things, even if some of them were still part of her dreams for the future.

'You remind me a little of my father,' she reluctantly admitted. 'He has the same level of dedication to his job.'

'Public service takes a particular kind of person.'

'Self-sacrificing?' she enquired.

'Mule-headed,' he replied.

'Oh, yes.' She nodded. 'He can be that, too.'

'You ever have the kind of talk with him that you had with your mother?'

Miranda angled her chin. 'Exactly how long were you standing outside that door?'

'Long enough to get the general gist. You'd think the doors in a place that old would be thicker.'

'In fairness to the door my mother does have a knack for getting me to raise my voice.' She rolled her eyes. 'In the olden days she'd have been described as unflappable.'

'Useful trait for a politician's wife.'

'True, but there's nothing worse than someone who won't argue with you when you're itching for a fight.'

'Might help if you were more open with her...'

'Now you're starting to sound like my father,' she complained. 'This is *so* not the conversation I planned on having with you the next time we were alone.'

'And now you're annoyed because you're not getting your own way,' he stated without missing a beat. 'Like I said—*hard work.*'

Miranda scowled at his profile. 'Did no one ever tell you it's okay to have the thought but it's not always okay to say it out loud?'

'Not much call for tact in my line of work.'

She shook her head and looked out of the windscreen as he steered them through the narrower side streets that fed into the main artery leading to the heart of Times Square. Speaking her mind wasn't something she'd been encouraged to do, especially when every word she said or Tweeted could be held against her. She'd always struggled with that. But with Tyler she didn't have to fight against her nature. It made sense of several things once she thought about it.

'Do you think if you were given more freedom you'd feel the need to go looking for trouble?'

The question made her sigh. 'I don't go looking for trouble. It has a tendency to find me.'

'Like a drugs raid in a nightclub,' he said dryly.

'How was I supposed to know the place had a drugs problem when I'd never been there before?'

'If you'd had an advance check it out they'd have told you.' When they stopped for a crossing light he looked her in the eye. 'There's an army of people at your disposal twenty-four-seven—never occurred to you to take advantage of their skill set?'

'I'm not going to bother someone every time I get the impulse to go out for ice cream.'

'It's your security detail's job to protect you,' he pointed out as bluntly as she'd learned to expect. 'You go skipping out any time you feel like it or get caught in the middle of a raid it makes both them and the department look bad. Wouldn't look a whole heap better for your father if he let something happen to you, would it?'

She wasn't trying to make anyone look bad. How could he not know that by now?

When the light changed and the last of the pedestrians on the crossing parted to make space for them to move forwards he surmised, 'You didn't think of it that way.'

'I suppose that makes me selfish?'

He shook his head. 'I don't think it's selfish to want time to yourself—I get that's what you were doing now. What I don't get is the reason you've stuck it out for so long if you don't enjoy it.'

Not true. 'There are parts of it I enjoy—meeting people, going places, supporting worthwhile causes.'

'So why not find a job that involves those things without the same restrictions?'

'I intend to. But I made a promise to my brother.'

She blinked. Had she just said that out loud?

'What kind of promise?'

That would be a yes, then. Briefly hiding behind the hand pretending to brush her hair into place, she checked to see how she felt about telling him. On a gut level it didn't feel wrong but there was a limit to how much she could say without delving into her family history. 'After abandoning him five days a week while I was at NYU I said I'd make sure he didn't have to smile for the cameras until the next election—he's due home the week before to help with the run-in. Win or lose, the plan was we'd make a stand together when he finished college.'

'What changed?'

'I did,' she answered truthfully before lowering her chin. 'I've never told anyone that. About the promise to my brother, I mean.'

'What about Crystal?'

'She wouldn't get it.'

'So why tell me?'

'Because I think you do.' Miranda lifted her chin and looked into his eyes as the traffic slowed. 'Like I said not so long ago—no one speaks to me the way you do. Maybe I needed someone to be frank with me so I could learn how to do the same in return.'

'If brutal honesty is what you need you're never gonna have to worry you won't get it from me.'

As much as it ruffled her feathers—particularly when he said something she didn't want to hear— she liked that about him. It was refreshing. 'You're never gonna let me win an argument for the sake of keeping the peace either, are you?'

'Nope,' he answered succinctly as he focused on the road ahead. 'And don't ever take me on in a sport unless you plan on losing.'

It was too good an opportunity to miss. 'Is there anything you're *not* good at?'

'Wouldn't you like to know?' he drawled.

When he turned his head the smile he flashed was so completely unexpected it stunned Miranda into silence. Enraptured by the sight she stared at the immediate change it brought to his face. His eyes were suddenly dozens of different shades of blue, the lines at the corners of his dense lashes deepening to give the impression there'd been a time in his life when he'd laughed often and loud. Added to the flash of pearly whites beneath the adorably crooked line of his lips, he wasn't just handsome.

He was irresistible.

Miranda felt her body and heart sway towards him with the same impulse as a flower turning its petals to the sun. She was smiling back at him before she realized she was doing it, her chest expanding with warmth.

But like all good things the moment didn't last.

When the SUV moved forwards again she decided it was probably just as well. She couldn't get more attached to him than she already was. So long as everything they did was treated as nothing more than foreplay she'd be fine.

Until she'd lived a little, explored some and quelled the doubts she had about her capability to do something worthwhile with her life, she couldn't so much as *think* about making a commitment to someone else.

Tyler Brannigan was a commitment kind of guy; twelve years on the job would have told her that even if he hadn't made the comment about wearing a wedding ring. From that point of view she was glad there wasn't any chance *he* would get more attached to *her*.

She just wished she knew why it made her feel so sad.

CHAPTER SEVENTEEN

A LIFE that involved posing on a red carpet wasn't one Tyler could ever see himself living. Considering the number of flashing cameras, it was a miracle she hadn't gone blind.

Posting up a few feet away from the spotlight, he watched her at work with a newfound respect. She seemed to know exactly where each lens was pointed; how to stand to display her stunning figure to its best advantage—though in fairness some folks were probably looking at her clothes— and throughout the test of endurance her smile never faded.

She was a pro. If she ended up supporting worthwhile causes when she had her freedom, they would be lucky to have her. The thought of her putting as much passion into her work as she did when she kissed him…

Well, suffice to say the world had better watch out.

When they stepped inside the movie theatre to

make way for the Hollywood stars she was equally adept at working the room. Some of the people she talked to he recognized, some he didn't, but she knew each and every one by name and managed to slip in several mayoral sound bites inside ten minutes. Since it was more than apparent he wasn't the only bodyguard present—some of them standing out like pro-wrestlers in a ballet class—he allowed her a little more space and stepped over to the counter nearby.

Her eyes sparkled when he returned. 'What is that?'

'Can't watch a movie without popcorn,' he reasoned.

'And a bucket of soda, apparently.' She smiled as they lined up to take their seats. 'You bought diet, right?'

'Not in this lifetime.'

Reaching out, she snagged a kernel of popcorn and popped it in her mouth.

'Did I say I'd bought it to share?'

She smiled brightly as she chewed.

It set the tone for the following hour and a handful of minutes. In the darkness of the auditorium, with numerous brushes of their fingertips in the search for popcorn, some of the tension seemed to ease from his body. He might have left the theatre feeling pretty relaxed if it hadn't been for the sex scene in the movie.

As the tension rose onscreen it seemed to coil around them. His senses became sharper and clearer. The seductive scent of her perfume, the contact of their elbows on the armrest between them, the saltiness on his lips he knew he would taste on hers when they kissed.

When his little finger brushed rhythmically into one of the groves between finer-boned fingers he glanced sideways and saw her press her knees together. His gaze lifted to the dark pools of her eyes; the thought her body was preparing for him immediately making his do the same in return. For a moment it felt as if they were the only people there. Then something was said onscreen that made the audience laugh, snapping him out of it and allowing him time to gather what was left of his senses before the credits rolled. But reminding himself of all the reasons he couldn't have her wasn't working. If anything it made the need for mutual release seem as vital as his next breath.

She tugged his sleeve to get his attention when they reached the foyer. 'Last time I was here, Mac thought it was quicker to use the side exit than wade through the mob out front.'

Tyler didn't argue, but when the door opened

there were almost as many people in the side street as there had been out front. The barricades were human—a line of uniformed police officers, some of them with outstretched arms, some as interested in who came out of the door as the crowd.

When Miranda appeared people started calling her name.

'I don't like this,' Tyler said tightly.

'It's fine,' she reassured him before pinning a smile in place and stepping forwards. 'Hi, how are you? Yes, it was great, you should go see it.'

While she worked her way down the line every instinct Tyler possessed screamed at him to get her out of there. He glared at one of the uniforms, tempted to get his badge number and report him for not doing his damn job.

As the door opened and a well-known talk-show host stepped outside the crowd yelled louder and moved forwards in a rolling wave that could barely be contained. His gaze immediately darted to Miranda. She'd got a couple of steps ahead and had her back to him. As he moved closer he saw her elbow move in a way that suggested whoever was holding on to her hand wasn't keen to let go. The minute he saw who it was Tyler grabbed the man's arm.

'Back off,' he warned.

'It's okay,' Miranda's voice said. 'I've got this.'

'I said, *back off.*'

The dark-haired man grimaced behind his glasses but didn't let go. When he raised his other arm and tried to put it around her waist Tyler's most basic instincts kicked in. Nudging her to the side to make room, he grasped fistfuls of sweatshirt and shoved the guy away from her.

'What are you *doing?*' he heard her say a split second before one the Hollywood stars appeared.

Suddenly the crowd was screaming and surging forwards. The guy he was holding stumbled backwards—was torn from his grasp—and Tyler was surrounded. Whirling around, he searched frantically for Miranda while his muscles clenched with the adrenaline-fuelled need to protect her. When he got a glimpse of her hair a second before her head dropped out of sight the thought of her being crushed almost made him lose his mind.

'Get out of the way!' he roared, shoving bodies aside until he could see her on the ground trying to get to her feet. Dropping down onto his haunches, he placed a hand on her shoulder and squeezed. 'You okay?'

She looked up at him and nodded, her eyes glittering with fear. 'I'm fine,' she lied.

Tyler pressed his forehead against hers for a moment, relief surging through his body. 'Let's go.'

Helping her upright, he took one of her hands in a firm grasp, his pace not slowing until he'd dragged her across Times Square and into the underground parking of the Hyatt. When they got close to the Escalade he turned around and hauled her into his arms. But instead of holding on to him, she struggled free and took a step back.

'Have you lost your mind?'

Tyler frowned. 'He wouldn't let go of you.'

'I was handling it.'

'It didn't *look* like you were.'

'You're putting me more on edge than those stupid letters,' she said with exasperation. 'How am I supposed to act normally if every time we go somewhere you freak out like I'm about to be kidnapped?'

'I suppose I should just stand there and let you get sucked into the crowd or *crushed.*'

She frowned back at him. 'What you should do is what everyone else who has surrounded me for the last eight years never learned to do—*ask me* if I'm okay.'

For the first time since he'd realized who she was talking to in the crowd Tyler stopped to think. Telling her it was the same guy he'd seen outside the school wouldn't help. He couldn't confess how uncharacteristically scared he'd been when he thought she might be hurt or how relieved he was when she wasn't, either.

So where did that leave him?

'You're right,' he admitted flatly, partly because she was but mostly because he couldn't think of anything else to say.

The admission took the wind out of her sails. 'Thank you.' She searched his eyes. 'Now do you want to tell me what happened back there?' When he didn't reply she took a short breath. 'Tyler, I'm trying to make an effort to communicate with you but you're gonna have to help me out here. I can't do it alone.'

He popped his jaw and tried to meet her halfway. 'Maybe I'm having a problem with the crowds.'

'Why?'

'Too many people.'

'We live in New York—it comes with the territory.' Her expression softened, the warmth of understanding in her eyes making him feel about two feet tall. 'It's because everywhere you look you're seeing potential dangers, isn't it?' She smiled. 'You don't have to worry about me. I've survived this long, haven't I?'

Tyler ground his teeth together. He'd liked it better when they were arguing.

'When I'm not appearing at public engagements I barely merit a second look.'

He very much doubted that. The night they met he would have picked her out of the crowd without any difficulty.

Stepping forwards, she took his hands and tangled their fingers together. 'I'll prove it to you.'

'How exactly are you gonna do that?'

'You have to trust me.' She lifted their arms out to the sides and briefly rolled her gaze towards the concrete ceiling. 'And possibly veer off the schedule a little bit…'

He didn't like where the conversation was headed any better than he liked the sensation he was being managed. 'Where are we going?'

'For a walk,' she replied with the same impossibly soft smile he'd seen her use on a small child.

'Not in Times Square, we're not.'

'I was thinking more along the lines of Carl Schurz Park.' Rocking forwards, she lifted her chin, her voice taking on the liquid cadence he'd been able to resist not so long ago. 'Seems to me we could both use the break…'

'Why there?' he asked while weighing up the pros and cons in his mind to distract his body from accepting the invitation she'd issued to kiss and make up.

'Because I've never got to see much of it beyond the view from my bedroom window. You can help me change that...'

Tyler finished the sentence for her when he realized what she was doing. 'And it's close enough to the mansion to set my mind at ease if you get mobbed.'

'I won't get mobbed,' she promised. 'You'll see.'

He'd been right; he *was* being managed. But while it was laced with thoughtfulness and a shared need to escape...

Flexing his fingers around hers, he lowered their arms to their sides and warned her, 'If I'm being played again, there'll be consequences.'

Just because it felt to him as if their relationship had changed didn't mean she felt the same way. He'd fallen into *that* trap before.

She fluttered her eyelashes. 'You promise?'

CHAPTER EIGHTEEN

As THEY walked side by side along paths that twisted and turned through theatrical staircases Miranda tried to enjoy the surroundings. It probably looked like Narnia in the winter with a blanket of snow on the ground, especially when the paths were lit by old-fashioned lamp posts. But even with her hand held in a reassuringly strong grip as soon as they were out of sight of the mansion, she couldn't relax. The incident outside the movie theatre had shaken her more than she cared to admit.

It magnified the sensation she should hold on to him but when she questioned if it was more than the natural reaction to a second reminder of the frailty of her body in comparison to his strength, she wasn't certain she wanted to know the answer.

They eventually got to the boardwalk where even with the FDR driveway beneath their feet it was easy to forget they were in the city. In silent agreement they headed to the railing. Sharing a few quiet moments of nothing—something she suspected was a rarity for them both—she smiled at the view. The thousands of square and rectangular windows lit up on the buildings across the river, the stars and moon above, the draped twinkling lights of the Fifty-ninth Street Bridge reflected in the moving water below.

It was magical.

Closing her eyes, she breathed in and caught a hint of the sweet scent of pipe smoke coming from some of the old men sitting on a bench to watch the last boats go by. Then—as if someone felt the need to add another layer of fairy dust— a harmonica started playing.

Opening her eyes, she tugged on Tyler's hand to draw him away from the railing. 'Dance with me.'

He shook his head. 'I don't dance.'

'Didn't anyone ever tell you that everyone should dance a little every day?'

'I don't sing into a hairbrush in front of the mirror, either,' he replied dryly as he allowed her to pull him into the centre of the boardwalk.

'How about laughing—you ever try that one?'

As they stilled he looked into her eyes and confessed, 'It's been a while.'

The returning hint of hollowness to his voice made her heart ache. Whatever had happened to him—the thing that made him so angry—wasn't something she could fix. But she could make an attempt at helping him put it to the back of his mind for a while.

'One arm goes around my waist like this...' Stepping forwards she moved the hand she was holding behind her back and released it. 'You hold this hand... I place this one on your shoulder... and we sway...'

She could feel the resistance in his body as she started to move. 'Don't think about it. Listen to the music—let it wash over you—and move your weight from one foot to the other.' When she felt him start to move with her a smile blossomed on her lips. 'It's like the ebb and flow of the tide. You're just a leaf in the wind...' When he lifted his chin her smile grew. 'The leaf was too much, wasn't it?'

'You could enjoy this a little less...'

She chuckled softly. 'I don't think that's possible.'

As they slowly turned in a circle she revelled in the luxury of being close to him and openly studied his face. Despite the times it felt as if she knew him better than she possibly could in such a short space of time there were others—like now—when she found him impossible to read. What was he thinking? Did the closeness feel as good for him as it did for her? Did he want her as much as she wanted him?

While he looked at her in a way that made it feel as if he could see her soul and held her with a gentleness that belied his strength it didn't feel wrong to trust him with her body. But before she did she wanted *him* to trust *her* and she wasn't certain he did yet.

Swiping the tip of her tongue over her lips, she took a short breath and decided to broach what she suspected was a difficult subject. 'If I talk to you about something you have to promise you won't freak out.'

'Meaning it's something I'm not gonna like.'

She searched his eyes before continuing. 'I think you know you can't go around intimidating people.'

'Not much call for good guys in the world I inhabit.'

Meaning he thought he wasn't one or he'd had to change to survive? She could have pointed out bad guys didn't come to a girl's rescue, share popcorn at the movies or dance with her in the moonlight, but instead she said, 'I'd have thought there was even more call for them there. At times lowering to the level of the people you deal with probably

seems like the only way you can make them understand you—it's dog-eat-dog, right?—but—'

'It's not how the people in your world behave.'

'You make it sound like we live on different
planets.'

'To all intents and purposes we do.'

She shook her head. 'I can't begin to imagine
some of the things you've seen.'

'You're not supposed to. It's why there are people like me doing the job we do. We're buffers.'

'Even soldiers in a war zone take the occasional
break from the front line. When's the last time
you did that?'

He frowned. 'That's been a while, too.'

Having spent more than enough time around
people in high pressured jobs to recognize stress
when she saw it, she'd thought it might be part of
the problem.

'Taking time for yourself—spending it with
the people you love and dancing every now and
again—wouldn't that remind you of what you're
fighting for?' When some of the tension returned
to his body she sought a way to make him understand what she was doing stemmed from the fact
she cared, even if it was more than she should.
'Haven't you ever had someone in your life you

looked forwards to seeing—who made everything you did and all the sacrifices you make worthwhile? You can't have gone this long without meeting someone like that. Everyone has a one who got away, right?'

The fist of jealousy that gripped her stomach made her hope the answer was no.

'Yes,' he replied.

Not that she wanted to know details but, 'Was your job part of the problem?'

'We both worked long hours.'

'What happened?'

'She married someone else.'

The information made her look at him with new eyes. Had his heart been broken? She wondered what kind of woman he'd fallen for and came to the conclusion she must have been pretty amazing. It left her with the sensation she had a lot to live up to—something her insecurities would play on if she let them. But if the woman had been dumb enough to let him go she couldn't have been *that* great. 'Was that when your work started taking over your life?' she asked.

'We're back to the subject of finding a balance.'

'Yes.'

'It's not always easy.'

'You think I don't know that?'

When he stilled she realized the music had stopped and turned to smile at the musician as he saluted them with his harmonica before walking away.

Tyler removed his arm from her waist and lowered their hands. As he led her back into the park he took a long breath and exhaled before asking, 'How did you know?'

'About the discrepancy in your work-life balance?'

'That I wouldn't hurt you that night in the alley...'

Miranda answered honestly. 'I just did. It was a gut-instinct thing. When something feels right it feels right.'

'You place that kind of faith in everyone?'

She arched a brow at him. 'After spending a quarter of my life surrounded by people who are never themselves around me— who laugh even when my jokes aren't funny or pretend to be my friend just so they can say they know me?'

'I'll take that as a no.'

Miranda stopped and turned towards him. 'Wait a minute. Are you telling me you *didn't* know?'

'No one knows what they're capable of till they're pushed,' he said flatly.

'Something pushed you before me, didn't it?'

The shadows between arcs of lamplight illuminating the path seemed to close in around him. 'Yes.'

Despite the dark tone to his deep voice her feet took a step forwards, her hand reaching out to the tense line of his jaw. When a muscle clenched beneath her fingers she wanted to reassure him nothing he said would change how she saw him—that when a person had the kind of faith she had in him it wasn't just for a minute or a day. She wanted to tell him that she thought he was strong enough to carry the weight of the world on his shoulders but he didn't have to. Not alone. But when it came down to it all she could manage was his name. *'Tyler—'*

'Don't.' A large hand covered hers and removed it from his face. 'We can't do that here.'

The rejection stung but somehow Miranda managed to rise above it and seek a rational explanation when she knew he wasn't immune to her touch. 'Has there been a noticeable rush of people who have recognized me? Why do you think so many famous people choose to live in New York?'

'You've made your point,' he replied. 'And I'm open to the idea of allowing more off-schedule walks to let you take a break. But we're still not doing that here.'

Frowning a little at the intimation she still needed permission to do what she wanted, she laid her palm on his chest, sidled up to him and cut her inner siren loose. 'Then take me somewhere we can be alone…and *get naked…*'

From her perspective, the sooner they started playing out a few of her fantasies, the better she'd feel.

'Not gonna happen.' Suddenly he was standing taller and straighter, his voice edged with fierce determination. 'I'm not interested in helping you stick a middle finger at your parents before you leave the family business.'

It was the closest she'd ever been to experiencing a slap in the face.

CHAPTER NINETEEN

THE second the words left his mouth Tyler regretted them.

When Miranda flinched it wasn't outwardly visible but he could see it in her eyes.

'You're trying to push me away again, aren't you?' she said with a hint of uncertainty that almost broke his resolve. 'It's what you do when someone gets close to you.'

He had to stay strong. Encouraging her anger would be better for both of them. 'I'm on the couch now, am I? Okay. I'll take a seat.' He moved over to one of the benches at the edge of the path, sat down and stretched his arms along the back. 'Don't you need a pen and paper to take notes for the rest of this therapy session?'

Miranda shook her head in a way that suggested she was disappointed in him. 'All you had to do was say you weren't ready to talk about it.'

Reminding him how close he'd come to spilling his guts wasn't the best tactic. 'What makes you think I'd talk to you when you have no idea how the world works?'

'If there weren't so many people trying to protect me from it I might have a better idea.' She arched a brow. 'You think I can't handle whatever you tell me?'

Good question. He knew she had guts and bravado. She'd demonstrated she had compassion, warmth and understanding. When added to her sensuality and the way she could turn him on with just a glance, it made him realize she was exactly the kind of woman a less tainted guy might want to build something with if things went well.

But the truth was it didn't matter if she could handle it. Simple fact was she shouldn't have to try.

Clearly seeking an explanation for what had gone wrong when they'd been getting along better she came up with, 'I'm certain getting personally involved isn't something you're encouraged to do during working hours.'

'What makes you think I find it difficult to avoid?'

She sighed. 'No one is that detached.'

'It's my claim to fame. Kinda like yours is being your father's mouthpiece by day and a closet rebel at night. That's what this is—' he lifted an arm to wave a forefinger between them '—another rule for you to break.'

'Deflection—you invented that, right?'

'I'm sure the mayor would be overjoyed to discover you're doing the nasty with one of your bodyguards.'

'What a delightful way to put it.' She lifted her chin a defiant inch. 'But even if I was, what happens between us has nothing to do with my family. It's not like this could go anywhere. They won't have to size up your suitability for a future son-in-law.'

Just as well, wasn't it? He could imagine how great he'd fit in at fancy dinner parties and how happy he'd be to traipse out his firstborn for the cameras. He'd create more negative publicity inside a couple of appearances than she had in years. 'Which is another part of the attraction, isn't it?'

'Unlike *someone* I could mention I didn't know who I was kissing that night in the hall. So what's your excuse for breaking the rules?'

'I needed a way to get you out of there before you were identified. It was the first thing that came to mind.' If he'd known how it would feel he might have thought twice, but when he tried to regret it, he couldn't.

'You hate that you're attracted to me, don't you?

I'm probably not even your type.' Her chin lifted another, more defensive inch. 'What was *she* like—your one who got away?'

When the thought she was jealous immediately made him want to reassure her she had nothing to worry about on that score, Tyler frowned. 'Not going there.' He pushed to his feet. 'This is just another example of you getting mad at me because you're not getting your own way.'

'That's not why I'm— You know what? I'm not going to be goaded into an argument with you. Back on the boardwalk I thought…' She clamped her mouth shut and shook her head. 'Obviously not—my mistake. I get it now.'

Tyler bunched his hands into fists at his sides so he wouldn't reach out to her.

He couldn't tell her that she was the first woman he'd danced with or that while he did he'd experienced his first moments of peace in longer than he could remember. He couldn't tell her when she'd asked if he had someone in his life he looked forward to seeing the first person he'd thought of was her. The number of things he couldn't say increased with each passing day. But they'd known each other for *two weeks*. Even if they had a future he wouldn't be telling her how he felt after two measly weeks.

What was next—a marriage proposal inside a month, quickie ceremony at six weeks and divorce a couple of weeks later? He wasn't that kind of guy. If he ever got round to putting a ring on a woman's finger it would stay there.

She rolled her eyes. 'I mean, how silly of me. You're obviously totally oblivious to me in that way. I could strip naked right now and you wouldn't even notice.'

The hell he wouldn't.

'I could date a string of guys while you're forced to watch and you wouldn't care. Better still, I could spend the night at their apartment while you stand outside the door and listen to every sound.'

The *hell* she would.

'Not that it would matter to you if I slept with every guy in the city…'

Something savagely territorial twisted hard in Tyler's gut. He'd kill every one of them with his bare hands.

'I could take every sex fantasy I've had about you since the night we met and try them out with whoever feels like getting down and dirty—'

That did it.

A single stride took him to where she stood. Then his hands were on her face and his mouth was on hers. There was nothing hesitant about it:

a brazen mating of lips and tongues that sent him up in flames. The pent-up frustration of the past week, knowing what it was like to touch her and being unable to do anything about it, was released in a flurry of kisses.

If they'd been within striking distance of a bed she wouldn't get to leave it until he'd shown her no other man would put as much effort into making her feel better than she'd ever felt before. He would find a way to brand her, bind her to him and make sure the world knew she was his, all the reasons he couldn't claim her forgotten in a red haze of desire.

'The things I said,' she mumbled against his lips. 'I would never do that to you.'

'I know,' he mumbled back.

The suggestion had been enough.

'I don't want you to think—'

'I don't.'

When he dropped his hands so he could wrap his arms around her waist and fit her soft curves to his body a moan vibrated in the base of her throat. 'You drive me crazy.'

Then they were even.

As he lifted his mouth to place worshipful kisses on her closed eyes and her forehead in an attempt to slow things down she sighed contentedly. 'Can we call the "who'll crack first?" competition a draw now and progress to the kissing marathon?'

Tyler brushed a waving lock of silky hair from her cheek, committing the softness of her skin to his memory. 'We don't have that luxury with your schedule.'

'We could try making time for it,' she suggested.

'How about we see how it goes for the next while?' Having stepped over every line he'd tried to draw between them bar one, it was the only concession he could make.

'I'm okay with that.' She rocked forwards onto her toes, crushing her breasts tighter against his chest as she lifted her chin and demanded, *'More.'*

Tyler was happy to oblige, picking her up off her feet as he slanted his mouth over hers.

After several minutes of kiss-filled silence she mumbled, 'You think I don't know you're carrying me back to the house right now?'

'If you'd shut up I could distract you better.'

'You can't carry me the whole way there.'

'Says who?'

Carrying her he could do. Looking after her while they were together he could do. Touching her and kissing her he could *definitely* do—wasn't as if he'd managed to stop himself from doing either one. Making love to her—no matter how desperately he wanted to—he still had to avoid. She'd thank him in the long run, especially if the alternative was living with the fact she'd given herself to a man who became a cold-blooded murderer.

He could protect her from that.

Even if it was the last honourable thing he did.

CHAPTER TWENTY

EITHER Tyler was more in control of the risk-assessment aspect of her security than she'd given him credit for or he was better at escaping than she'd ever been. Not that it mattered after two of the happiest weeks of her life.

Every time there was so much as the smallest gap in her schedule he would take her somewhere she'd never been. An impromptu concert tour of some of the best musicians performing in subway stations; to partake of lunch from a street vendor and run back to the SUV through the rain when the heavens opened; people-watching in parks where they could pit his detective skills against her imagination in games of 'guess the profession.'

It was a bittersweet romance.

Each place he showed her made her fall deeper in love with the city she called home and broke her heart a little when she realized how much living she'd missed. Add stolen kisses, forbidden touches and lingering heated looks to the mix and her only complaint was he hadn't found a gap in her schedule for sex. It was something she planned on fixing if he wouldn't. A girl had to do what a girl had to do.

When the suggestion was made they spend time together on a rare day off from campaign duties she thought they were finally headed for an afternoon of debauchery. But when they pulled up outside a neatly kept house in Staten Island her rising anticipation was replaced by surprise.

'This is where you live?'

It looked more like a family home than a bachelor pad.

'It's where I grew up.' He switched off the engine and unbuckled his seat belt. 'Hope you're hungry. There's always enough food to feed an army at Sunday lunch.'

Miranda froze. 'Wait. *What?* I can't meet your family.'

'You can sit out here if you want but you're gonna be here awhile.'

She'd never felt more in need of an escape route. 'I can go for a walk or take a ferry ride. I've always wanted to do that. I'll meet you back here in a couple of hours.'

'In what universe do you think that's likely?'

'It's your *family*. I can't go in there.'

'You meet people every day. I'm not seeing the problem.' He leaned across and opened her door. *'Out.'*

'I can't.'

'Yes, you can.'

'Would it make a difference if I said please?'

'No,' but it earned an all-too-brief brush of his firm mouth across her submissive lips. 'I got a call last night to say there's some big family announcement I'm not to miss and, since I can't get out of it, you get to be here. We'll be an hour, two tops, and then—if you're a very good girl—we can take a ride on the big orange boat.'

When he added a push of encouragement to her shoulder, Miranda chose to get out of the car rather than fall face-first onto the street. She stared at the house as she walked to the sidewalk, anything resembling an appetite replaced by the kind of churning that made her pray she wouldn't throw up on one of his relatives.

'How are you going to introduce me?'

'I don't know how rich folks do it in Manhattan high society.' He reached for the latch on the gate. 'But here on Staten Island we tend to use names.'

'I can't believe you're doing this to me.'

'It's not that big a deal.'

Yes, it was. How could he not know that—did they have to have the relationship definition talk? Maybe she was overthinking it. Maybe he brought dozens of women home.

The thought made her frown.

'Think of them as potential voters if it helps,' he said as they got to the top of the porch steps. 'But I should probably warn you most of them like the look of the other guy.'

She sent him a withering look.

When they stepped into the hall he took her coat, hung it on a rack and called out, 'We've got company.'

Persuaded around the corner with a large palm on the inward curve of her spine, Miranda discovered four pairs of curious eyes studying her. Standing there stark naked couldn't have made her feel more exposed.

'This is Miranda,' Tyler announced.

A woman with long dark hair and soulful brown eyes was the first of them to step forwards and hold out a hand. 'I'm Jo. It's nice to meet you, Miranda.'

'And you.' She smiled apologetically. 'If I'd known where we were going I'd have brought something with me—I feel terribly empty-handed.'

'Soon fix that.' A tall man who was obviously

one of Tyler's brothers stepped forwards and shook her hand the second Jo let go. His vivid blue eyes narrowed a little. 'You look familiar.'

'My husband, Danny,' Jo explained before nudging him in the ribs. 'She's the mayor's daughter, you idiot.'

'Nah, that's not where I know her from...' A slow smile spread across his mouth. 'How's your Southern accent?'

It took a second but when she made the connection Miranda's eyes widened. He'd been one of the police officers in the hallway; more specifically one of the officers who had caught her making out with Tyler while pinned against a wall. There was just never a giant hole in the ground when a girl needed one, was there?

Danny winked as he let go of her hand. 'Don't worry, your secret's safe with me. *You,* on the other hand—' he pointed at his brother '—are gonna have to buy my silence for at least the next decade.'

'You open your pie hole your lovely wife will end up wearing black,' Tyler warned.

Jo linked arms with her husband and patted his chest. 'You can tell me later, babe.'

'You already know.'

'How about you remind me?'

As they moved away Miranda dropped her chin and aimed an accusatory glare at Tyler. 'You didn't mention your brother was there that night.'

'Didn't I?'

'No.'

'Uncle Tyler!'

Her eyes widened as a small child launched herself at him and was swung into the air. 'You have a niece?'

'Indeed I do.' He smiled indulgently. 'Hey, Munchkin, who's the best-looking guy in the room?'

'Daddy,' the girl replied with conviction.

Tyler glanced briefly at Miranda. 'They can get a bit confused at four.' He bounced the child higher in his arms as he walked away. 'Remember we talked about this? Let's go over it again...'

The image provided such a contrast to the dangerous man she'd seen in an alley Miranda couldn't quite equate the two as she watched him disappear into what she assumed was the kitchen. But the reminder of how gentle he could be was a powerful aphrodisiac.

Why weren't they at his place having sex?

'Amy adores him,' Jo's voice said beside her. 'I think it's because at times they're the same mental age.'

Detective-Takes-The-World-Too-Seriously-To-Dance had a Peter Pan side to his personality? Miranda blinked. She *really* wanted to see that. 'Is she yours?'

'No, we've only been married a few months. She's Johnnie's daughter. He's the eldest. Then—in descending order—there's Reid, Tyler and Danny. Liv is the youngest.' She smiled when Miranda looked at her. 'I know. It can be a lot to take in on the first visit and I'm afraid they're not even all here yet. Liv and Blake are running a little late with their big announcement—my money's on baby news. Reid is undercover so we haven't seen him in a while—makes it twice as important for everyone to be here if it is baby news, y'know? Momma Brannigan is in the kitchen.' She leaned closer and lowered her voice to a conspiratorial whisper. 'But don't be scared. She's lovely.'

While she blinked at the overload of information Jo smiled and linked their arms at the elbows.

'Let's get the rest of the introductions out of the way. It's easier a few at a time.'

After meeting Johnnie and his wife Miranda swiped her palms over her hips and asked, 'Can I help with anything?'

'You can give me a hand setting the table if you tell me where you got those gorgeous shoes.'

A conversation about fashion and Jo's cheery chatter helped distract her until Tyler reappeared with an older woman. 'My mom,' he supplied as he set down a platter of food on the table.

'I guessed.' She stepped forwards and reached out a hand. 'It's a pleasure to meet you, Mrs Brannigan. Thank you for allowing me to visit your lovely home.'

Sky-blue eyes sparkled with humour as she looked up at her son. 'Is she always this polite?'

'No,' he said flatly.

'How do we get her to stop?'

'Couple of minutes in my company usually does it.'

'Then you'd best stay with her.' She patted his arm. 'With any luck some of it might rub off.'

Tyler nodded firmly. 'Knew that was coming…'

The interaction made Miranda smile. When he smiled crookedly in reply, her heartbeat stuttered and skipped a couple of beats. Dragging her gaze away, she reached out to straighten the cutlery on the place setting closest to her. The desire to ravish him and be ravished in return was at the very least wildly inappropriate in front of his family.

'We're here!' a woman's voice called from the hall.

Another round of introductions ensued and, despite some odd looks when Tyler placed her in the chair next to him for lunch within a short space of time Miranda fell a little in love with the rest of the Brannigans. They interacted like a single unit, at times talked over each other in a way that made it difficult to follow the flow of conversation, but what she found most fascinating was how different Tyler was with them.

She'd never seen him so relaxed, heard him express an educated opinion on so many subjects or realized how funny he could be when he set his mind to it. It gave her a glimpse of how he must have been before he saw too much. For the life of her Miranda couldn't imagine why the woman he loved had let him get away. To be loved by a man like him, to have children with him and spend her life standing by his side, being there when he needed her and knowing he would do the same in return...

A wave of longing overwhelmed her. Nothing had ever seemed more beautiful or more terrifying.

Understandably it made her more aware of the happy couples surrounding them as the meal finished and she helped with the clearing up. She looked at Jo and Danny as he tucked a strand of dark hair behind her ear. The intimacy of the touch and the heat in his eyes made it obvious Tyler's younger brother was very much in love with his wife. The feeling was just as obviously returned. They made it look as if there were no one else in the room but them. It was incredibly romantic but, since it also made her feel as if she was intruding on something private, Miranda tore her gaze away.

Inevitably it was drawn to where Tyler was leaning against the archway to the kitchen. She smiled as she ran a cloth somewhat aimlessly over the table. Even when sporting a basic blue-jeans-and-sweater combo he was devastatingly handsome. She watched as he cradled a mug of coffee in his hand, his expression pensive. When he blinked dense lashes she followed his gaze and discovered he was looking where she'd been looking. Jo laughed at something Danny said and as Miranda's gaze returned to Tyler the corner of his mouth lifted and his expression softened.

'*What happened?*' she'd asked.

'*She married someone else,*' he'd replied.

Miranda's heart twisted, a brief frown aimed at the woman she'd liked so much. How could she do that to him? Marrying his brother was bad enough, flaunting her happiness in front of him was unforgivable—and she'd seemed so *nice*.

Immediately crossing the room, she stood close enough to feel the heat radiating from his large body, her back to everyone else as if she could somehow shield him from pain. '*She's* your one who got away?' she whispered.

Tyler dropped his chin and frowned, his deep voice equally low. 'Don't make me regret bringing you here.'

'She's your brother's *wife.*'

'She wasn't always his wife. Leave it alone.'

'But how can you—?'

He shook his head and glanced around. 'Just this once do you think you could do what I tell you to do?'

When he looked into her eyes again what she thought she could read in the cobalt depths made Miranda want to march across the room and give his sister-in-law a piece of her mind. She understood how difficult it was for Tyler to be there even if no one else did. Had he brought her along as back-up or a smokescreen? She was a lot happier with the first option, would have volunteered if she'd known he needed support. Didn't he know that? She wanted to talk to him about it—hear the story from beginning to end in his words—but it was the archetypal wrong time, wrong place.

He lifted his mug and drained the contents. 'You want to take that ferry ride, we best say our good-byes.'

Miranda acquiesced with a nod. A ferry ride would be the ideal place to talk. She just wished she didn't feel as nervous about hearing what he had to say as she'd been about meeting his family. Gathering herself together, she pinned one of her public-persona smiles in place and turned around. Even if it was more than likely she would never see them again she wanted his family to think well of her.

One by one the people she barely knew said their goodbyes with a hug, a kiss on the cheek or both. At first she felt awkward about hugging them back, her body stiff and unyielding; particularly with Jo. But by the time she got to the eighth person—his mother—she was holding on for a moment longer than strictly necessary, her throat clogged with emotion.

They made her feel so accepted it was all too easy to paint a picture of a fantasy future where she was part of their world. She would sit in the seat next to Tyler every Sunday, at Thanksgiving and Christmas, and be there just for him the way it felt he'd been for her.

She gave herself a mental talking-to as they left

the house. If she wasn't careful before she knew it she'd be doodling Miranda Brannigan inside hearts on stationery. The man had been in love with another woman—still was for all she knew. Then there was the small matter of her freedom—she didn't want to trade one form of captivity for another.

Their relationship was about *sex* and, once they'd had a little chat on the ferry to ensure they were on the same page, they were going to his apartment to have lots of it.

CHAPTER TWENTY-ONE

IF PRESSURED Tyler might have admitted taking Miranda home to meet his family wasn't planned. But it would have taken extreme torture for him to confess the reason behind it was that it felt as if she had him on the ropes.

Truth was he doubted taking her to meet the family priest would keep them out of the bedroom for much longer.

As she walked beside him, unruly tresses of flame-red hair tossed by the wind, all he could think about was how it felt to have those silky soft strands sliding over his fingers. He wanted to strip her naked and keep her that way until he'd sated his hunger for her. He wanted to map her body with his mouth and his tongue, taking her close to the edge over and over again without allowing her release until she begged him to take her.

He'd used every trick he could think of to get it off his mind. He'd even summoned random pages of books from his memory and recited them word for word inside his head. When his talent for retaining information chose to remind him of the time he'd furtively flicked through a copy of *Lady Chatterley* during puberty, he'd stopped.

So much for *that* great idea…

But there was no point denying there was something else going on that had nothing to do with sex.

He'd watched from the sidelines as she smiled, talked and laughed with his family. She'd looked right there—as if she belonged—and Tyler realized on some level he'd known she would. What he *hadn't* realized was how much he would like having her there. He'd even looked at Jo and Danny and felt at peace with the past; as if things were the way they were supposed to be.

It felt as if a weight had been lifted.

Studying her from the corner of his eye, he tried to figure out what was different about her—the thing that allowed her to work such a miracle. But when she looked at him and flashed a small smile he was distracted by the sensation something was off.

'You okay?'

She avoided his gaze and nodded. 'I'm fine.'

'Did I ever mention one of my detective skills is the ability to spot a lie?' Tyler raised his hand

and waggled a forefinger over his shoulder. 'Hairs on the back of my neck stand up.'

'They all hugged me.' She shrugged a shoulder, her tone deceptively dismissive. 'I'm not used to that.'

It made him want to sit her parents down for a little chat. Didn't they know their daughter *at all?* Would it be such a damn hardship for them to *get to know her?*

They obviously needed someone to tell them what they were missing.

Dropping her gaze to the ground for a moment, she took a short breath and asked, 'How long has it been since your father passed away?'

'Nine years. He had a heart attack.'

Her voice softened. 'I'm sorry.'

'It happens.' Tyler shrugged. 'Work hard, play hard—that was his motto. I doubt he had many regrets.'

They crossed the street to the boardwalk before she commented, 'You were different with them.'

'So were you.'

'I don't usually meet families.' She scrunched her nose a little. 'I mean, I do, but…'

'But?' he prompted.

'It was different this time.'

Tyler was about to ask why when he glanced ahead. 'Can you run in those shoes?'

'They're not exactly designed for running.'

'Try.' He took her hand. 'Ferry's in, we gotta move.'

They were the last people to board before it departed. Miranda looked up at him with sparkling eyes and flushed cheeks, so beautiful she was making it difficult for him to look anywhere else. When she laughed he smiled back at her. Every time she did that it made him want to be a funnier guy so he could coax the sound from her lips.

'Can we stand outside?' she asked breathlessly.

'You'll get cold.'

She shook her head. 'I don't care.'

Guiding them to what shelter he could find at the end of the deck, he watched her reaction to the new experience as she caught her breath from the run. He drank in her animated expression, the way her eyes sparkled with delight, and as always wondered how it felt to see the world through her eyes. The little adventures they'd taken might have been an attempt to keep them out of the bedroom but they'd done more than that. At least they had for him.

He saw the city with fresh perspective. It wasn't tarnished by cynicism or taken for granted the way he normally did. As a result he'd thought about the small part he played in the greater scheme of things and come to the conclusion a little was better than nothing. One less perp on the streets was one less crime—several in the case of repeat offenders. If it meant she was safe when she began to explore on her own he'd arrest each and every one of them in her name.

'They liked you,' he told her, in case she didn't know. 'That's why you were treated to the hug-fest.'

'I got the impression your family would make anyone you brought home feel welcome.' A soft smile came through in her voice. 'You're lucky to have them.'

'They're not bad,' he allowed. 'Probably a bit late to trade them in.'

'It can't have been easy for your mom with five little kids running around.' She waited until he looked into her eyes. 'You're all quite close in age, aren't you?'

'Arrived in an eight-year bonanza of adorability.'

'That kind of time frame would terrify me.'

'My great-grandmother had eleven.'

Her eyes widened. 'Seriously?'

'It's why the Irish never have to invade a country. We infiltrate.' The comment had the desired effect: she laughed. But Tyler shook his head when it was followed by an involuntary shudder. 'I said you'd be cold out here.'

'I don't want to go inside.' When the wind blew a lock of hair across her face, she raised her hand to brush it back and looked over the water again. 'This is amazing.'

Releasing her hand, Tyler took a step forwards, folded the edges of his jacket around her narrow shoulders and wrapped his arms around her body. 'Better?'

She settled in as if she'd always been there, her arms around his waist and her cheek against his chest. 'Much.'

He rested his chin on her head as they sailed past the Statue of Liberty.

'She's humongous.'

Tyler looked down at her with amusement. 'How can you *not* know that?'

'She looks smaller from farther away.'

Fair enough.

'Did you tell her how you felt?'

It didn't take a genius to work out they weren't talking about a national monument any more.

'I thought she knew.'

'She might not have married Danny if she knew.'

'No.' He'd accepted that long before he came to terms with it. 'Anyone who sees them together knows they're good for each other.'

'Can't be easy to watch.'

'Wasn't for a while…' A guy could come up with a lot of reasons not to attend Sunday lunch when he needed to, but that would change now, thanks to her.

'No one else figured it out?'

He sincerely hoped not—because that wouldn't be at all awkward—but realistically all he knew for certain was, 'You're the first person to bring it up.'

There was a palpable moment of hesitation before she asked, 'Do you still love her?'

Not in that way. He wouldn't be standing there with her if he was in love with someone else. He wasn't wired that way. 'Part of me will always feel something for her. Just because it didn't work out the way I thought it would doesn't make it any less real.'

'Why didn't you tell her?'

And there it was: the million-dollar question.

When he didn't answer she leaned back and looked up at him. 'You don't know?'

'We were friends. I didn't think she was ready

to hear it, but the fact is I never knew why until recently.'

'You don't want to tell me,' she surmised.

Considering some of it had to do with his attraction to the woman he was with, not so much.

'Do you regret it?'

He looked into her eyes. 'It's history.'

'You want to change the subject,' she said. 'Okay. What are we doing—you and me, Tyler and Miranda?'

'What do you think we're doing?'

'I thought it was foreplay,' she answered frankly. 'Neither one of us is interested in making a commitment, are we?' There was a beat before she added, 'We enjoy each other's company—most of the time—and you know I want you.'

He did. Even if he couldn't see it in her eyes, he could hear it in her voice. Her tone was liquid as she said the words, thick with sensuality and more potent than any drug. Resisting her was the equivalent of a slow, painful death, every muscle in his body straining towards her.

'I know *you* want *me*.' Her lips formed a decadently sinful smile. 'Some things are hard to hide…'

To prove the point she brushed her stomach across his abdomen in a deliberately provocative move. Tyler sucked in a sharp breath through clenched teeth, unable to stop his body from reacting. She had that effect on him even without trying. When she put effort into it he didn't stand a chance. He dropped his hands to her hips to hold her still.

'What do you want me to say?' he asked tightly.

'I don't want you to say anything. I want you to take me to your apartment, take me to bed and take me.'

He'd never wanted anything more. 'I can't.'

'Why not?'

'It's not that simple.'

'Yes, it is.'

He wished it were. 'You need to think this through.'

'You think I haven't?' Removing one of the arms around his waist, she snaked it between them and raised a hand to set fine-boned fingers against his jaw as she looked deep into his eyes. 'I haven't thought about anything else since the moment I laid eyes on you.'

Utilizing every microscopic fraction of resolve he had left, Tyler removed her fingers. 'We can't do this.'

'Look me in the eyes and tell me you don't want me.'

'I'm not gonna lie about that.' Not after she'd so ably demonstrated his weakness.

'Then what is the problem?' There was a brief flash of fire in her eyes. 'In case you hadn't noticed I'm throwing myself at you. That doesn't happen very often.'

Some of his frustration bubbled to the surface. 'Damn it, woman, I'm trying to do the right thing here.' He glanced over her head to see who was watching what they were doing, his fingers tangling with hers at their side. 'You're not making it any easier.'

'And I'm not going to until you can give me a rational explanation for why this can't happen when we both want it to,' she said on a note of exasperation.

'I won't take advantage of the situation.'

'Uh...*hello*...woman willing to be taken advantage of over here.' She lowered her voice. 'I want to have wild, uninhibited sex with you. I want to feel your hands on my body. I want...' she rocked forward and pressed her breasts against his chest '...you to make me *scream* your name...'

Tyler swore viciously beneath his breath. He'd said *he* was more trouble than *she* could handle? *Man* was he ever outclassed on that score. Every strand of knuckle-dragging caveman that remained in his DNA demanded he tame her and tie her down. But the part of him that had made the mistake of looking for something more meaningful in the wrong place wouldn't let him take her without it.

He wanted to strip her naked in more ways than one. He wanted to climb inside her mind and discover all her secrets. He wanted her to be more herself with him than she'd ever been with anyone else. He wanted sleeping together to mean something to her because he knew it would mean something to him. But he couldn't say any of those things without discussing a future he couldn't plan until after the day of reckoning.

From what she'd said it didn't even look as if she wanted a future with him. Then he remembered she'd *asked* about commitment. It hadn't been a statement of fact. The devil was in the detail. Where there was a loophole, there was a way in. He needed to know how she felt and in the absence of words he knew how to get to the truth.

Making the first connection with their eyes, he dropped his guard and allowed her to see how much he wanted her. It drew a low gasp from her lips, encouraging him to continue despite the glimpse of fear he got in return. Running his hand over her back in a soothing caress, he cradled her close, releasing her hand so he could brush the backs of his fingers over her cheek.

'What are you doing?' she whispered.

He angled his head and lowered his mouth to her lips. 'Don't speak, just feel.'

Moving his hand, he pushed her hair over her shoulder, changing the direction of his lips at the last possible second to place a kiss on the sensitive skin of her neck. He slid his mouth upwards, circled the shell of her ear with the tip of his tongue and felt a shiver run through her body.

'Tyler—'

'*Shh...*'

He kissed his way down her jaw and captured her mouth, alternating between soft and hard, breathless and slow. While she responded in kind he could sense she was holding back, conflicted by the desire to have him take her hard and fast the way he knew she wanted him to and the warm, cherished feeling he was attempting to convey with tenderness. Then she was leaning into him. The kiss became deeper, richer, full-bodied and intoxicating, creating a haze around them that blocked out everything else.

Something he didn't recognize expanded in his chest. It pushed the air from his lungs and filled the cavity until it felt as if it would break his ribs and burst free. In seeking out the truth about how she felt he'd touched the edge of something so large within himself he couldn't see to the other side. But before he could figure out what it was, with no more warning than a low moan she wrenched her mouth free and took a sharp step backwards.

'*Stop.*'

When he looked at her Tyler discovered her eyes were wide with anguish. He frowned. What had he done wrong?

She sucked in a sharp breath and shook her head. 'This isn't what we're meant to be doing.'

'I thought you wanted to make love,' he said roughly, the after-effects of the best kiss of his damn life still rippling through his body.

'I want us to have *sex.*'

'Meaningless sex.' The empty, emotionless joining of bodies that led to a brief, unsatisfying climax held zero appeal for him. He didn't want that with her.

'No.' She frowned back at him. 'I mean, yes, but not *totally* meaningless…something somewhere in the middle… I don't know… I don't have much— that's not the point!'

A surge of affection lifted the corner of his

mouth. 'Might need you to explain that a little better...'

'Don't look at me like that.'

Suddenly she was more scared than he'd ever seen her look before—even when she saw him roughing up a low life in an alley.

'Come here.' He took a step forwards and reached out to draw her back into his arms.

She took a step back and left her hands at her sides. 'We're not *dating*,' she said firmly. 'You don't have to spoon on the romance to get me into bed.'

'We're not having a quick roll between the sheets, either,' he replied with equal determination. 'If that's what you're looking for it's a deal-breaker. We do this, we do it my way.'

'Which is what, exactly?'

His reply got stuck in his throat, what he wanted to say suppressed by self-doubt. He'd known Jo for *years* before he thought he felt something more— had debated telling her for months and ultimately was glad he hadn't. If he was wrong again, if he'd misjudged, if the day of reckoning came and he was too far gone to haul himself back from the gates of hell—

'What kind of game are you playing?'

The tremor in her voice tore a hole in his gut.

'I'm not playing a game,' he replied flatly.

'I won't be your rebound.'

'You're not.'

She was clearly confused—and she had every right to be. Her gaze frantically searched the air above his head. Then it slammed into his, her tone heavy with suspicion. 'Are you doing this to control me and keep me in line?'

He flicked a brief glare her way. 'I'm gonna let that one slide 'cos I know you have trust issues.'

'You were given the talk, weren't you?'

Tyler frowned again. 'What talk?'

'The talk Lou Mitchell gives to all the new bodyguards at the mansion about boundaries. It never occurred to me before but now it makes sense…' Fire blazed in her eyes, incinerating her fear. 'What did he say to you?'

Tyler froze when he realized what she meant. He wouldn't lie to her but if it was taken out of context—

'What did he *say?*'

The rise in her voice drew the attention of some of the people at the other end of the deck.

'You need to calm down,' he said in a lower voice.

'I'll calm down when you tell me what he said.'

No, she wouldn't. Not if she didn't let him get

it all out. Hauling in a deep breath, he took a run
at it. 'He said to do whatever I had to do to—'

'*Wow.*'

'I'm not finished.'

She laughed sarcastically. 'Oh, you've said more
than enough. Congratulations.' Her hands lifted
in front of her body to reward him with a round
of applause. '*Well played.*'

Tyler popped his jaw. 'Miranda—'

'How do I get off this damn boat?'

It might have been something that worked in his
favour if they hadn't been so close to Manhattan.
When she yanked open the door and headed inside, he followed her. 'We need to talk about this.'

'No, we don't.' Her gaze searched for exit signs
as an announcement was made about their arrival.

'You haven't got the full picture.'

'Believe me, it's in high definition.' She spun
on her heel and marched towards the other end of
the boat. 'I won't be manipulated by you or anyone else.'

He reached for her elbow. 'I'm not manipulat-
ing—'

Yanking her arm out of his reach, she swung
on him with enough ice to freeze boiling water.
'Don't. Touch. Me.'

Tyler was about two seconds away from losing

it. 'We're gonna talk about this whether you like it or not. But not here.'

'We're done talking.' She angled her chin with blatant contempt. 'And don't worry—you won't have to give up any more of your precious time to amuse me as a reward for good behaviour. Just be thankful you didn't have to prostitute yourself to get the job done. But then you never intended to cross that line, did you? Everyone has their limits.'

'Step too far with that one, princess.'

'You're *fired*.'

'You can't do that.'

'I just did.' She smirked and turned away, using her hundred-watt smile to flirt her way through a group of tourists to the front of the line.

When the rest of the passengers moved forwards he had to push his way through, his gaze firmly fixed on a head of flame-red hair. 'Excuse me. Sorry. Coming through…' He had to jog a little in the terminal to catch up. 'Still trying to cut me loose?'

No reply but she picked up the pace.

Tyler simply lengthened his stride. 'Long walk back to the mansion from here.' He nodded when she lifted her chin. 'Okay. Silent treatment is fine with me.' He held open a glass door for her and followed her outside. 'I'll talk. You listen.'

'Go to hell.'

'That the best you've got?'

She stopped dead in her tracks, turned, took a step forwards and swung a palm at his face. He caught her wrist in midair, glared at her from the corner of his eye in warning and then loosened his grip when he saw the horror of what she'd almost done in her eyes. It was a strategic mistake because the second he did she twisted it free, shoved both hands into his chest and caught him off balance. His heels caught on the kerb behind him and the next thing he knew he was sitting on his ass in wet grass.

Planting her fists on her hips she angled her chin and snapped, 'Is *that* better?'

It caused the kind of life-changing epiphany Tyler hadn't seen coming. For a moment he simply stared at her in shock. Then a vibration started in his chest, moving upwards into the base of his throat. The sound was rusty from lack of use, but familiar.

'You choose *now* to laugh?' She shook her head in disbelief. 'You're a twisted individual.'

When she spun around and marched to the edge of the road to hail a cab Tyler scrambled to his feet and jogged after her to try a more persuasive tone. 'If you let me tell you the rest of the sentence we can clear this up.'

'I don't want to clear it up,' she retorted. 'I want you to stay away from me.'

'You don't want that any more than I do.'

The convulsion of her throat gave him an indication of how hurt she was, instantly causing him pain in response. 'You don't care what I want.'

'You couldn't be more wrong about that.'

It made her glance sideways at him as a cab pulled up but she didn't look him in the eye. 'Don't follow me.'

He frowned. 'Where do you think you're going?'

'*Home.* Not that it's your problem any more.' She lifted her chin again. 'I have three weeks left to serve on my sentence. Once they're done I'm going to go out into the big wide world, find the first available guy who'll spend time with me because he wants to and not because he's being paid to do it, and I'll have meaningless sex with him until neither of us can stand up.'

'No, you won't,' he said with conviction while the words stirred another savage streak of territorialism. 'We've already had that talk.'

'Wind up a mechanized toy, you shouldn't be surprised when it keeps moving after you set it down.' She frowned when he placed a palm on the top of the door to stop it from opening. 'Let me go.'

'I'm going to,' he said reluctantly before taking a step closer. 'But only to give you long enough to calm down. When you're thinking clearly and have questions you know how to find me.' He gave her something to mull over. 'You might want to make one of them why I kissed you the way I did.'

Pushing against his palm, he stood tall, dropped his arm to his side and watched her get into the cab. As it left it felt as if part of him went with it, but he guessed he would have to get used to that.

When his phone rang he waited a few moments before answering it. 'Brannigan.'

'You wanna go on a stake-out?' his partner enquired.

Tyler's blood chilled. 'You found him?'

'Maybe…' There was a brief pause. 'Turns out your friend Jimmy has been worrying enough about being seen as a snitch to become one.'

'I'm on my way.'

CHAPTER TWENTY-TWO

THE club encompassed a city block with a dance floor, live DJ and a seating area for private parties at the back. Despite the fact it was a Sunday night and many of them had work in the morning, it was packed with a hip Manhattan crowd of twenty-to-thirty-somethings.

Miranda was at the bar with Crystal. She'd bought the first drink to sip while she tried to calm down. When it had the same medicinal effect associated with a stiff brandy she ordered another. The numbness that set in with her third was more welcome than any of the little umbrellas lined up side by side would ever know.

There were four of them now, not counting the one in her glass. They were pretty. She'd decided to see how many colours she could collect.

'You know what *really* bugs me?' she yelled over the music. 'By allowing me to throw myself at him like some kind of desperate woman he made me feel *needy*. I don't do *needy*. If I was *needy* I'd sleep with every guy who showed an interest in me.' She waved a limp-wristed hand in the general direction of the man hovering nearby. 'Like that guy over there. He's cute and he's been smiling at me for the last ten minutes.'

'He's the bartender and you've been tipping him the price of your drink every time you buy one,' Crystal said dryly while attempting to take the cocktail glass from her. 'I think that's enough alcohol for you, young lady. You never could hold your liquor.'

When Miranda moved the glass out of her reach some of the liquid splashed over her hand. 'If you weren't trying to take it off me, I wouldn't be spilling it.' She scowled. To solve the problem she downed the colourful contents. 'I love this song. Let's dance. I want to dance.'

'We should probably get you home—or to my place for coffee. Coffee would be good.'

'I don't want coffee and I'm not going home. I want to have *fun*.' When the screen of her cell phone flashed on the bar beside the empty glass she picked it up and squinted at the caller ID. '*Ugh,* he just can't take a hint, can he?'

'He won't be happy when he finds you like this.'

Miranda rejected the call with a flourish and set her phone down. 'I don't *care*.'

'Yes, you do. That's half the problem.'

'*He* doesn't care. He's only spending time with me because it's his *job*.'

'And there's the other half…'

She blinked. 'Is there something *wrong* with me?'

'Of course there's not,' Crystal said with conviction. 'You're a beautiful, sexy woman. Any guy would want you. Have a glass of water.'

'I thought he wanted me as much as I want him. I mean, when he kisses me—*wow*—and when he touches me—*boom!* Fireworks, y'know what I mean? He makes me. *So. Hot.* But does he follow through, even when he has permission to…' she made speech marks in the air with her fingers '*…do whatever he needs to do to keep me out of trouble?*' She rocked back and announced, 'He's a tease. I didn't think guys did that.'

'Who knew?' Her best friend nudged the glass a little closer. 'Take a sip, it's very refreshing.'

'It should *not* be this hard to get laid. Do you know I don't even know what an orgasm feels like with company?'

The comment earned a somewhat blurry-around-the-edges expression of interest. 'I did *not* know that. And it's a conversation we'll be having when you're sober. One little sip for Auntie Crystal, there's a good girl…'

'I bet when he gives a girl an orgasm it knocks her socks off. Not that I'm likely to find out any time soon. No toe-curling bliss on the horizon for me. Being the mayor's daughter is like wearing a *giant chastity belt.*'

'Would you prefer fizzy water?'

'And what the hell was he thinking taking me home to meet his family?' She swallowed the lump in her throat. 'They're wonderful. Did I tell you how wonderful they are?'

'About a half-dozen times...'

'Can I get you ladies another drink?' a voice said beside them.

Crystal smiled sweetly. 'I'll give you twenty bucks to shake your cute little cocktail shaker elsewhere.'

'They're exactly the kind of family I'd like to have some day,' Miranda continued. 'I love the whole meeting-up-for-Sunday-lunch thing.' She sat a little straighter. 'But we're not a *couple.* I don't want to *fall in love with him.*'

'Are you?'

'Am I what?'

'Falling in love with him...?'

'*No!*' she replied vehemently before taking a beat. 'Maybe... I don't know... I don't *want* to be.'

'How come?'

The tears she'd been battling since she left the ferry terminal threatened to break free, forcing her to take several deep breaths before she replied. 'Because then I'd belong to him and I'd really like him to belong to me for a little while.' She flicked her hair over her shoulder. 'I don't want to talk about this any more. It's depressing. If you love me, you'll dance with me.'

'I do and I would.' Crystal glanced over her shoulder. 'But I have a sneaking suspicion you're about to be carried out of here...'

Miranda twisted around, lifted her gaze and frowned. 'Go away, Tyler. I don't *like you.*'

His gaze shifted. 'How much has she had?'

'Too much,' Crystal replied. 'Not that it takes much to begin with—she's always been a cheap date that way. I've been trying to get her to go home for the last half hour.'

'I'll take it from here.'

'Go easy on her. She's hurting for a reason.'

'I know.'

Miranda shook her head in disbelief and regretted it the second the room began to spin. 'That's it—go right ahead and talk about me like I'm not here. Start making decisions for me and you'll both be like everyone else in my life who doesn't give a crap about how I feel.' She raised her arm high above her head and waggled her fingers. 'Hey, *cute guy,* drink me!'

'You've reached your limit,' Tyler said firmly as he lifted her cell phone and took her elbow. 'And you're gonna apologize to Crystal for that in the morning. Thanks for the heads up on her location.'

The last part made Miranda gasp. 'You sent for him? How *could you?*' Taught her not to leave her cell phone on the bar when she went to the restroom, didn't it?

At least Crystal had the decency to look apologetic. 'Because it's not me that you need to be talking to right now and you'd never forgive yourself if you made it into the papers this close to Election Day.'

'Up you get,' Tyler ordered.

'I'm not leaving.'

'Yes, you are.'

'Make me.'

'Okay.'

When he bent down and tossed her effortlessly over her shoulder, Miranda struggled. 'Put me down!'

'Bye, Crystal.'

'Bye, Tyler.'

'Stop him!' she yelled at the bouncer on the door before hiccupping. 'I'm being kidnapped!'

'No, she's not.' Tyler simply rearranged her weight to flash his shield. 'NYPD.'

'Isn't that the mayor's daughter?' the bouncer asked.

'She's one of those lookalikes,' Tyler said as he walked away. 'Been conning free drinks all over town…'

'Put me *down!*' Miranda repeated while she was carried down the sidewalk. 'Women *hate it* when guys do this.'

He muttered a reply that sounded as if it included the words 'worked for' and 'Brannigan' and 'when he did' before raising his voice to inform her, 'You're gonna have the hangover from hell in the morning.'

'Why should you care?' she asked his broad back.

'The thought I might scares the life out of you, doesn't it?'

She lifted her chin. 'What's that supposed to mean?'

'You're a flight risk. I knew that at the start. What I didn't know was why.'

'But you think you do *now?*'

His head nodded against her flank. 'This is what you do when things get too much—you run away to find solace in having fun. Up till now it's been the life you didn't want and how claustrophobic you felt. This time it's me.'

Miranda spluttered, 'Arrogant much?'

'This isn't you. You're more than this.'

'You don't *know me.*'

He took a deep breath she felt against her legs. 'You're an amazing woman with the potential to do equally amazing things with her life. Is this how you're gonna deal with your problems when you're forty? Whether you like it or not I do care so when you're ready to talk about what's bothering you let me know.'

'I already tried that,' she said in a smaller voice.

'No, you didn't. You ran away.'

The truth silenced her while he set her on her feet. Swaying a little she pushed her hair out of her eyes and looked up at him. Damn him for being so big and strong and bulletproof. She *hated* that he could make her feel so small and weak and vulnerable. She didn't want to fall for him.

It would be so much simpler if she wasn't.

When her lower lip trembled she bit down on it.

The pad of a thumb stilled the movement. 'Don't do that. You'll make it bleed.'

The husky edge to his voice twisted her heart into a tight little ball. She didn't want tenderness from him. Not if he was going to take it with him when he left. 'You're looking at me the way I don't like again,' she complained.

He shouldn't make promises with his eyes he wasn't prepared to keep. But what was worse was how it made her *feel*. At the beginning he excited her—he still did—but along the way he also surprised and challenged her, making her re-evaluate her life and what she wanted from it. She would do it—she would give up her freedom to be with him.

She would give up *everything*.

How had he made her feel that way in just a few weeks?

His thumb brushed across her cheek before he dropped his hand to his side. 'Let's get you home.'

Miranda allowed him to move her around so he could open the door and help her inside. She gazed at his profile as he leaned in to click her seat belt into place, saw him glance at her from the corner of his eye and wished she knew what to say. How was she supposed to tell him what she'd felt when he kissed her—lost and found, hopeful and hopeless, joyous and afraid? It was so many things at once.

It felt as if she belonged in his arms. But he'd had an opportunity to correct her when she said neither of them wanted to make a commitment and he hadn't. It wasn't his fault she'd discovered she wanted something more. The thought of her life without him in it *sucked*. When she'd thought he was only spending time with her because he had to the ground dropped out from under her feet.

It had hurt. *So. Much.*

She hauled in a ragged breath and blinked when her vision blurred. As she did long fingers closed around the hand in her lap and she lowered her chin, watching as she turned her palm into his. She loved holding his hand but if she had one wish it would be to hear him laugh again so she could take the time to appreciate the sound. She'd waited so long to hear it. What if it never happened again?

If they just had a little more time…

'Will you tell me the rest of the sentence?' she asked in the same small voice as before.

Tyler didn't need an explanation, the deep rumble of his voice washing over her in a soothing caress. 'He said to do whatever I had to do to keep you safe because you don't know how vulnerable you are in the spotlight.'

'That's not true.' She attempted to smile through her tears. 'I've always been vulnerable in the spotlight. I used to get stage fright. Threw up every time I had to appear in public—got reminded of it when we went to lunch today. I was scared people would find me lacking in any one of a dozen different ways. Not smart enough, funny enough, pretty enough or dressed well enough. It's why I took the part in the play during senior year in high school. I figured if I tackled my confidence issues head on...'

When her voice trailed off he squeezed her hand. 'People love you within minutes of meeting you. I've watched it happen.'

'They don't have to spend much time with me.'

'Well, there is *that*.'

Miranda chuckled, hiccupped and then sniffled before leaning back against the headrest. She didn't realize she'd fallen asleep until she was being carried up the stairs of the mansion in a much more romantic position. Snuggling closer to his neck, she took a long breath of Tyler-scented air and sighed contentedly. *This* she could definitely learn to live with. Being protected from the world wasn't so bad the way he did it. He even took her shoes off and tucked her into bed.

When he disappeared without saying anything she tried to lift her heavy head to see where he'd gone. Then the mattress dipped beside her, a fingertip brushed her hair off her forehead and he was leaning over her.

Looking deep into his eyes, she tried to re-member what her life was like before he walked into it. Considering it hadn't been that long ago, it shouldn't have been difficult, but all she knew was how alone she'd felt without him, how overly defensive she'd been when she discovered he was her bodyguard, how much she'd loved their little adventures and that she owed him an apology for knocking him on his ass. She couldn't believe she'd been angry enough to hit him.

What must he think of her?

'Why do you put up with me?' she asked.

'You're cute when you're drunk.'

'I'm more trouble than I'm worth.'

'We'll debate that one another time.' He trailed his fingers along her cheek and watched the move-ment with one of his more intense gazes. 'Go back to sleep.'

'Stay with me?' she whispered. It was a loaded request but she couldn't stop herself making it.

'I can't. Even if we weren't in the mayor's house, I had to leave a stake-out to come rescue you.' He drew in a long, measured breath and slowly ex-haled. 'I gotta go back. There's something I have to do. If it doesn't turn out so great…' He frowned before looking into her eyes. 'Just remember if I had a choice, things would be different.'

Miranda smiled sadly. It felt like a goodbye.

She didn't want him to go.

'Don't forget that,' he insisted.

'I won't,' she promised.

His gaze roamed over her face before he leaned down to press a kiss to her forehead. 'Go back to sleep.'

Miranda ran her palm up over his chest. 'I'll see you tomorrow, won't I?'

He smiled the crooked smile she loved so much. 'You fired me, remember?'

'You're rehired.'

'Go to sleep.'

Stretching upwards, she wound her arm around his neck and lifted her chin. 'I'm not sleepy any more.'

Tyler sighed heavily, his voice laced with regret. 'I was hoping you wouldn't say that.'

Something cold and metallic snapped around her wrist.

Miranda twisted her head on the pillow so she could see what he was doing. 'What is that?'

The restraint was unyielding as he closed a second loop around one of the iron rungs on her bedstead.

'If you'd fallen asleep I wouldn't have to do this.' He got to his feet. 'Water's beside you. I don't have any aspirin or I'd leave that, too. You're gonna need it when you wake up.' He bent over and lifted a washbowl off the floor to wave it at her. 'You can use this if you need to be sick or feel the call of nature.'

'It's an *antique*.'

'Then you better not break it.'

The outrage she felt was the equivalent of downing a dozen cups of espresso, the effects of the alcohol wearing off pretty damn fast as he walked away.

'You can't leave me like this.' She lowered her voice to snap, *'Tyler!'*

'I'll leave the key for Grace. She's usually in before everyone else.'

And then he was gone.

Flumping back onto the pillow, she lifted her chin to glare at the handcuffs and rattled stainless steel against iron. How was she supposed to explain *that* in the morning?

She was going to kill him the next time she saw him.

CHAPTER TWENTY-THREE

BY THE time Tyler returned to his partner and the rookie detective who'd been attempting to fill his shoes, the stake-out wasn't a stake-out any more. 'Can't believe you were gonna start the party without me…'

'ESU just got here. You haven't missed anything.' He frowned. 'Where's your vest?'

'In my locker,' Tyler replied. 'Tell me it's him.'

He wanted the day of reckoning out of the way so he knew if he had a future to plan.

'Arrived on the heels of a large shipment—we've got him this time. There's nowhere to go.'

As they silently approached the warehouse with their weapons drawn Tyler forced any thoughts of Miranda to the back of his mind. He knew she was safe, that had to be enough, even if he regretted not telling her how he felt when he had the chance. It was better he hadn't, he reasoned, especially now.

The raid was textbook, communication made

with hand signals to place everyone in position before a countdown of fingers indicated when ESU would break down the door. Once they were inside it went equally smoothly—Tyler's voice joining the others to identify them as cops to the gang of men unpacking boxes. As they raised their hands in the air his gaze searched their faces and shifted in time to see a couple of men disappearing into the back.

Tyler ran after them, slowing his pace when the chase led into abandoned machinery and piles of empty crates.

His partner caught up to him. 'You see them?'

'Not yet.'

They split up, working as one to search high and low.

'One over there.' Tyler pointed when he heard a noise and saw a figure too short and stocky to be the man he was after. 'I've got the other one.'

'Don't do anything stupid.'

The warning fell on deaf ears, the dark side to his nature taking over as he stalked his prey. Tyler didn't fight it. He welcomed its arrival, embraced it and challenged it to do its worst. It was the only way he would know how far he could go. To fuel the need for revenge he summoned the image of a broken body to the front of his mind, saw the unnatural position of her limbs and thought about how much she'd suffered.

Then he rounded a corner into a narrow alley of crates and saw Demietrov standing a few feet away.

A slow, cold smile appeared on the man's face.

Tyler frowned, the gun wavering a little in front of him. Restlessly shifting his weight from one foot to the other, he locked his arms into place and looked down the barrel with determination. He could feel the weight of his finger resting on the trigger, but even when looking his nemesis straight in the eye he couldn't take the shot.

Something wouldn't let him.

When he spoke his voice rang around the empty space with the kind of conviction that came from doing the right thing. 'Andrei Demietrov, I'm placing you under arrest for the trafficking of illegal substances and the suspected murder of Candice James.' The darkness shrank within him, folding in on itself until it became the manageable part of his personality it had been before his life got so screwed up. 'You have the right to remain silent—'

As he stepped forwards the man reached out and tumbled the nearest pile of crates to the ground, creating a domino effect that forced Tyler to jump out of the way before he continued the chase. There was the sound of a door slamming shut. When he got to it and swung it open he discovered it was raining outside. He checked each side of an arch of security lighting and took a step forwards…

The impact knocked him backwards a second before he heard the shot and felt a searing heat blaze through his shoulder. There was another shot in quick succession—he felt a second burn in his upper arm—and then there was a hail of gunfire and a body slumped onto the ground. As he staggered backwards Tyler knew he hadn't fired his weapon. The ESU guys had done what he couldn't.

Sickly warmth soaked his shirt as his back hit the wall beside the door and his knees gave out.

He stared at the body as his partner appeared and swore succinctly while prying the gun from his hand. 'This is Detective Ramirez, we have an officer down—I repeat, officer down. I need a bus at—'

As he rhymed off the address—presumably over the phone—Tyler felt a sense of peace wash over him. When it came down to the wire he didn't have it in him to murder a man in cold blood. Maybe he wasn't as far gone as he'd thought.

Maybe Miranda had pulled him back from the edge. He tried to focus past the pain while the warmth drained from his body. Getting shot hurt like a bitch. And he'd left Miranda handcuffed to her bed.

A rumble of laughter made him groan.

'You want to share the joke?' his partner asked as he took a look at the damage.

'The one time I don't wear a vest...' he mumbled back.

'Murphy's Law...you're Irish...work it out.'

Tyler swore when he added pressure to the wound on his shoulder. 'Don't think that'll help,' he gritted through clenched teeth as his vision blurred. 'I think that one went through.'

'Here's hoping. If it's gone through they won't have to dig it out. What about your arm?'

'That one they'll have to dig out.'

'Just as well you're right-handed, isn't it?'

Tyler frowned. A few feet back, to the side of the ESU's tactical guys as they checked the body lying on the ground, a silent figure stood in the pouring rain. Her face wasn't covered in blood any more and she was smiling at him. How could she be happy he'd failed her—wasn't the whole point of haunting him to keep him focused on avenging her death? 'I'm sorry.' It was the first time he'd told her that. 'I screwed up.'

'You've got nothing to apologize for,' his partner replied, obviously under the impression Tyler was talking to him. 'Can happen to the best of us.'

When he blinked the raindrops off his lashes Candice was replaced by another woman with long dark hair and while she was smiling, too, she was also shaking her head. Why was he seeing Jo? She wasn't dead. He blinked again, the movement taking more effort than it had before.

'Stay with me,' his partner's voice said.

A woman with tumbling tresses of flame-red hair appeared in Jo's place and even in the rain Tyler could see she was crying. His heart twisted. She should never have to cry because of him, even if part of it was alcohol related. He wanted to make her happy, hear her laugh every day and see the fire in her eyes when they argued. He didn't have to keep his foot on the brake any more. The obstacles standing in their way weren't insurmountable. If they were then he wouldn't feel the way he did.

Not that he had any control over it.

'Stay with me.'

She'd said that, too, and he'd never wanted anything more. If they'd been born in an earlier time he'd happily keep her barefoot and pregnant and protect what was his, keeping them safe from marauders. He'd have been good at that. All the touchy-feely modern-day stuff that said a guy was supposed to embrace his feminine side and emote, not so damn much. Tyler didn't have a feminine side. Karl Jung could take his theories on human psychology and—

'Ty, snap out of it.' A hand smacked his cheek a few times. 'You gotta stay awake.'

Damn, it was cold. He should have worn a jacket. Screw the jacket, he should have worn his damn vest and then he wouldn't be ruining a perfectly good sweater.

'Anyone on your team an EMT?' his partner yelled at the ESU guys. 'Get him over here!'

Excellent—someone else to fuss over him. Anyone would think he was the first person in the world to get shot.

'I'll call your family when we get to the emergency room,' his partner said in a lower voice.

'You do that I'll kick your ass.'

'Anyone you *do* want me to call?'

'No.' Since shaking his head took too much effort, he frowned again. 'Don't want to worry her.'

'We all need someone who does that.'

'You'd like her.' His voice slurred.

'Can't be that good a judge of character if she likes you…' His partner moved to make room for someone else. 'We need to stop the bleeding.'

'I'm on it,' a voice he didn't recognize said. 'Stay with us, brother.'

With his eyelids growing heavy Tyler used up some of his waning energy on what probably looked like a sappy smile. He didn't know what he'd done to deserve it but she did like him. Unless he was very much mistaken—and he prayed he wasn't—she liked him a whole heap. Way he saw it she was his—he just had to find a way to make her believe it, too. Jo hadn't been his one who got away. But if he was dumb enough to let Miranda go without putting up one hell of a fight she would be.

They just needed a little more time….

'Stay awake, Ty. Where the hell's that bus?'

It was the second time in less than twenty-four hours he found his ass on wet ground while he wondered when he'd fallen for her. The first had been the 'there you are' moment that identified her as the one he'd been waiting for all along. He'd even laughed with joy. She was the reason he'd been emotionally unavailable to other women. She was the reason he hadn't told Jo how he'd thought he felt. At times she drove him nuts but she was smart and funny and gutsy and sexy as hell. It shouldn't have been such a great surprise he wanted to hold on to her. Any guy would. But they could forget it. She was *his*.

'Tell her,' he mumbled.

'Tell her what?'

Somewhere along the way she'd got under his skin and crawled inside, filling him up until everything else was pushed out. It didn't matter if it was too soon or that there was still so much for him to learn about her. It was just there…like air…without it…

He couldn't breathe.

'Ty, come on, man, you gotta hold on.'

He hadn't known love could be so…*big*. He felt crushed under the weight of it. If he knew she could feel the same way it would lift him up higher than he'd ever been before. But until they got a chance to talk he just needed a little nap—he had to be at full strength to fight for her. Forty winks should do it.

With sirens sounding in the distance she was the last thought on his mind as he passed out.

CHAPTER TWENTY-FOUR

MIRANDA opened her eyes and groaned as she squinted at the bright light shining through a crack in the curtains. When she turned over to check the time on the alarm clock the handcuffs snagged her wrist.

'Damn it, Tyler.'

The three gentle knocks on her bedroom door echoed inside her head as if they'd been made with a demolition ball. 'Grace?' she asked tentatively.

The door opened a crack. 'Can I come in?'

'Yes.' Miranda fought embarrassment as the older woman crossed the room. 'Tell me there's a key in that envelope.'

'With a note which said to bring this…' she held out a bottle of aspirin '…and that you'd probably want a bucket of coffee…'

'You have *no idea.*' She took a deep breath while Grace negotiated the lock on the loop above her head. 'You're probably wondering what's going on.'

'I don't need an explanation.'

Miranda held up her arm when it was freed from the bed. 'You have a soft spot for him, don't you?'

'Well, he is handsome...'

'Yes, he is.'

'And you have been happier in the last few weeks...'

When the second loop opened she rubbed her wrist. 'Yes, I was.'

Grace studied her face with knowing eyes. 'I wouldn't give up on him yet. A man doesn't handcuff a woman to a bed to keep her safe if he doesn't care.' Setting the handcuffs on the bedside cabinet, she lowered her voice and smiled with a rare glimpse of mischievousness. 'Not that there aren't other things you could do with them...'

'Grace.' Miranda gasped. 'I'm shocked.'

'No, you're not.' She chuckled as she turned away. 'I'll have them bring breakfast to your room.'

'Wait.' Swinging her legs off the bed Miranda stood up to fold her in a grateful hug. 'You know I love you, right? I don't say it enough.'

Having been—what had he called it, treated to a hug-fest?—she wanted more hugs in her life. When Tyler was gone she would need them.

'You don't have to say it. You're the daughter I never had.' Grace leaned back and winked. 'Now make me proud and go give that handsome devil hell for what he did to you.'

'I will.'

The thought lifted her spirits a little and by the time she'd showered, had breakfast and was feeling more human she'd made a decision. There was no point dwelling over how little time they had left. If all they had was a few more weeks she was going to make the most of them. He did care—if she'd been thinking sensibly she'd have known that without him saying it. She had to accept that was enough, even if she struggled with it. But she didn't want a marriage proposal or a drawer at his apartment or even to keep a toothbrush in his bathroom. All she wanted was to continue seeing him. Maybe she should tell him that?

If it didn't feel like the biggest step she'd ever taken with the most massive gaping cavern for her to fall into if he didn't feel the same way, she might consider it.

She checked her watch and frowned. Grace was late with the itinerary. It wasn't like her. Lifting her things, she decided to meet her at her desk, the sight of someone she hadn't expected making her footsteps falter when she got there. 'Lewis. I didn't think you were working today.'

'I wasn't.'

Miranda's gaze shifted when Grace appeared from her father's office, the grim expression on her face creating a sense of foreboding. 'What's going on?'

'We don't know much yet,' she replied in a low voice. 'But it's all over the news. Apparently Detective Brannigan was on some kind of drugs raid last night and—'

'*No.*' The word parted her lips on a tortured whisper.

Grace reached out a hand and squeezed her arm. 'He's all right. Your father has asked me to find out what hospital he's in so we can send a gift.'

'What happened?'

It earned another squeeze—one that didn't loosen—which suggested she knew Miranda would need the support.

'He was shot.'

Grace had been right; she did need the support. Her body swayed, a wave of nausea rising in her throat. It was her worst nightmare. She couldn't bear the thought of him lying bleeding somewhere while she'd been sleeping. But falling apart wasn't going to help.

The only thing that would was seeing him.

Making a conscious effort to prick the bubble of shock surrounding her body, she summoned strength she didn't know she possessed and took charge. 'Lewis, bring the car to the door and use your connections in the department to find out what hospital he's in. You'll find out quicker than Grace.'

He nodded as he left.

'I need you to reorganize today's itinerary,' she told Grace. 'Most of the morning involves listening to speeches so they can do without me but there's a scheduled visit to a veterans' association before lunch. Give them a call and see if we can move it back a couple of hours. If we can't extend my apologies and see if we can reschedule for later in the week—tell them I'm sick if you need to.'

'I'll see to it. What do you want me to tell your father if he asks where you are?'

'Tell him the truth. If he has a problem he can discuss it with me later.'

'I'll call you with an update.'

Between several calls, a check on the internet for what little news there was and with Lewis driving with the lights flashing on the front grill of the SUV, they reached their destination in relatively good time.

Standing at a nurse's station, she announced, 'I'm looking for Detective Brannigan's room. I was told it's on the fifth floor.'

'Are you family?'

'He's my bodyguard.' She lifted her chin. 'I'm Miranda Kravitz. My father is the mayor.'

Meaning if the woman got in her way she would have a fight on her hands…

'Do you think you can get him to stay in bed?'

The question made her sag with relief. If they were having difficulty keeping him in bed it was a good sign. 'Point me in the right direction and I'll give it a try.'

'Third door on the left,' the woman replied. 'Good luck. You're going to need it.'

After pausing beside the open door to draw a deep breath of air into her lungs, Miranda crossed the threshold and took an inventory with her eyes. He was sitting on the end of the bed, frowning at a navy T-shirt as he tried to find a way of putting it on one-handed. Under normal circumstances her gaze would have snagged on his bare chest and marvelled at the sight of smooth skin stretched over taut muscle. Instead it was drawn to the squares of gauze taped to his upper arm and below his shoulder. If the second square had been a few inches lower the bullet would have punctured a lung.

She swallowed the jagged lump in her throat to ask, 'What do you think you're doing?'

His gaze lifted, a brief flash of surprise crossing his face before his voice rumbled, 'It's called escaping. You of all people should know that. How did you get here?'

'Lewis brought me. I didn't give him a choice.' She crossed the room and set her bag down on an empty chair. 'And you're not going anywhere. What did the doctor say?'

'That they dug out the bullet, replaced the blood I lost and stitched up the holes.'

'And that you should *rest,* right?'

'Look, I get what you're doing but if you want to do something useful you can get me the hell out of here before my family comes back. If I have to endure another candlelit vigil around this bed I'm gonna jump out that window. My mother is *this far away...*' he raised the hand holding the T-shirt to demonstrate the distance with a small gap between his thumb and finger '...from getting Father Mike to drop by and bless me.'

'They're worried about you,' Miranda argued in their defence, ignoring his obvious frustration.

Tyler lowered his hand, frowning at the T-shirt again as he held it at arm's length and tried to shake it straight. 'If it wasn't for one of Danny's ESU buddies flapping his jaw none of them would have known.'

'Well, it's nice to know I wasn't the only person you didn't think merited a phone call.'

His hand dropped onto his lap. *'Miranda—'*

'If the doctor says you're supposed to stay in bed—'

'I can do it at home.' He looked up into her eyes. 'I don't need anyone's approval to check out. They can put a note on the form to say it's against medical advice if they're worried about covering their asses.'

Her eyes narrowed. 'Why do I get the impression this isn't your first visit to a hospital?'

'Me and Father Mike go way back—broken leg when I was nine, first concussion when I was twelve...'

She arched a brow. *'First* concussion?'

'I read a lot. When I was a kid it made it feel like I had something to prove when it came to sports. Get me out of here and you can examine every inch of me for scars.'

'Promises, promises,' she muttered before accepting the inevitable. There was no way he was staying put, but if she couldn't stop him leaving she could make sure they took every possible precaution. 'You're not leaving until I've talked to your doctor and he's prescribed pain medication.'

Tyler stood up. 'I don't need any.'

Again with the something to prove, but the lines of strain at the corners of his eyes and the rigid set of his jaw suggested otherwise. She folded her arms. 'I have a vehicle and a driver who can take you straight home. Do you want help to escape or not?'

Surprisingly he took a moment to mull it over, his gaze searching the air before he lifted his hand. 'You can start with helping me put on a T-shirt. I've been swearing at this thing for the last five minutes.'

Miranda noted the way he avoided looking at her and got the sense he wasn't happy with her being there. It hurt that he wasn't—especially when she'd been so desperate to see him. But she wasn't there for totally selfish reasons—she wanted to be there *for him*. If he'd let her...

'In order for me to do that you have to sit back down...' She looked at the T-shirt as she took it from him, noticed something behind it and shook her head. 'Let me guess. You gave up swearing at the button on your jeans five minutes ago.'

Determined she could touch him impassively while he was injured, she stepped forwards and folded the T-shirt over her forearm to free up her hands. But it wasn't her reaction she should have worried about. The second her fingers folded around the waistband of his jeans—the backs of her fingers brushing against warm skin—he sucked in a sharp breath and tensed. Her gaze darted upwards and tangled with his, the mixture of heat and pain in his eyes making her grimace.

'Sorry,' she whispered.

'Don't be,' he gritted back before the heat in his eyes intensified to drown out the pain.

Miranda slipped the button into the loop and removed her hands. 'Sit.' She lifted the T-shirt. 'Bad arm first...'

The eye contact was broken to allow her to negotiate dressing him with as little discomfort as possible, but when the task was complete he forced her gaze back to his by capturing her wrist.

'I'm fine,' he said firmly.

'No, you're not.' Her voice trembled a little on the words. 'You got shot. With a *gun.*'

'Technically speaking I got shot with bullets *fired* from a gun.' A corner of his mouth tugged when she frowned. 'Still here, aren't I?'

A landslide of the emotions she'd been burying

tumbled down on her, hammering her heart into a bruised ball of pulp. She'd known he would leave soon but if he'd *died*...

He was so much more than she was. While she'd slept off the alcohol she'd consumed in a bid to escape reality he'd been on the front line, protecting the city. He'd dedicated his life to making the world a safer place without seeking anything in return. How could a man like him ever love a woman like her? He deserved so much better.

Lifting her free hand, she ran trembling fingers over his short hair and down the back of his neck. He closed his eyes in response—what looked like agony crossing his face before he opened them. She wanted to take away his pain and soothe the tension from his body. She wanted to take care of him, listen to the things that troubled him and put his needs above her own. She wasn't any good at cooking or cleaning or doing laundry—doubted she would ever fill the role of domestic goddess— but she was willing to *try.* If there was anything she could do to make his life easier she would put her heart and soul into it. She just wished she thought she could be happy that way.

Even if she hadn't already planned to find something that could allow her to make a difference to people's lives, getting to know him would have inspired her. The irony was they could probably have teamed up. One of the charities on her short-list dealt with victim support…

'You know this means I'm not your bodyguard any more.'

She stared at him. The thought hadn't occurred to her.

As her hand lowered to her side he explained, 'They'll make me take time off. If I'm lucky I'll get desk duty in a week but I won't be back on tour until after the election.'

Miranda felt the time that had meant so much to her slipping through her fingers. She twisted her wrist free and took a step back, turning away to pack what few things he had into the open sports bag on the bed beside him. His family must have brought what they thought he needed. They had the right to do that. She probably shouldn't even be there. Purposefully keeping her tone light, she told him, 'You'll heal quicker that way.'

'And you'll be busy with the campaign.'

'I will.' If he was trying to let her down easy there wasn't any need. She'd known a day would come when he wouldn't be there any more. She was just thankful he would be *somewhere*— could take comfort from that while spending the rest of her life trying to make him proud to say he'd known her. 'It can get hectic in the last few weeks.'

'When it's over you'll be free.'

'I'm looking forward to it. I've made a lot of plans—things I want to do, places I want to see.' Silently clearing her throat, she lifted her chin and informed him, 'I'm going to check in with your doctor. Lewis should be up in a minute. Then we'll take you home.'

She headed for the door.

'Miranda, *stop.*' The forceful edge to his rough voice froze her feet to the ground. 'Don't run away this time.'

Pinning a bright smile in place, she turned around to give the performance of a lifetime. 'If I was running away I'd take my bag. It's Gucci.'

Tyler frowned and angled his head a little to study her from the corner of his eye. 'Are you still mad at me for the handcuffs?'

'You did what you felt you had to do.' She shrugged. 'I'd probably have done the same thing in your shoes.'

He opened his mouth, sucked in a breath and hesitated. It wasn't like him but in the blink of an eye he recovered, his voice laced with determination. 'We need to talk.'

'Now?' she asked with as innocent an expression as she could muster. 'I thought you wanted to leave?'

'You rearranged your schedule to be here, right?'

'Grace did.'

'How much time did she get you?'

'I'm visiting veterans after lunch.'

'What about tonight?'

Since she wasn't convinced prolonging the agony would make it feel any better Miranda lied. 'I'm pretty solidly booked for the next few weeks. We could meet up for coffee after the election if you like. You have my number.'

'Still trying to cut me loose, aren't you?'

'You're not my bodyguard any more.'

'So that's it. There's nothing you want to say to me.'

'Of course there is.' She sighed, struggling to keep up the pretence. 'You've watched over me all this time, put up with *a lot* and I've enjoyed our time together. I can never begin to repay you for—'

Tyler shook his head. 'I shouldn't have left the keys with Grace. That was a mistake. Go find the damn doctor so I can blow this joint. But if you think we're done here you can forget it.' He pushed to his feet. 'Just be thankful I'm not in any shape to toss you over my shoulder again.'

She blinked. 'I don't get why you're angry.'

'Well, when you figure it out let me know.'

When he turned and started an argument with the zipper on the sports bag, Miranda took a step forwards. 'Tyler—'

He lifted the bag and marched past her. 'I'm going to sign the paperwork.'

The silence in the car on the journey to his apartment was deafening. He left with a curt 'thanks' and not so much as a sideways glance at her. It was awful. She'd never felt worse—empty and alone and facing an endlessly long Tyler-less future. It was over. He was gone.

Miranda would never know how she kept her facade in place for the rest of the scheduled itinerary. But at the end of an interminably long day it took its toll.

She dropped onto the edge of her bed, deflating like a balloon losing air. When the tears came she didn't stop them. There was nothing remotely dainty or feminine about it when the floodgates opened, either. When she lay down on the covers heaving sobs racked her body until her face was mottled and her eyes were red and swollen. Later, when she hauled herself upright and made it under a hot shower, she turned the water on to high and cried some more while its warmth did nothing to remove the chill from her body.

It was late when she was reduced to sniffling into her pillow. Staring into the darkness, she started to think things through. She thought about the first time he took her hand; how big a pain in the ass he'd been when he blocked her escape attempts; how he'd been the first person to be brutally honest with her; how the most dangerous man she'd ever met could make her feel safe and protected. Then she thought about the night in the alley, the shudder that ran through his body when he held her, how he resisted the kiss but wrestled control from her. From that point of view he'd always had the upper hand. When he kissed her nothing else mattered but kissing him back. At least it hadn't until her heart got involved.

Then something happened. Somewhere in the middle of her sentimental journey to revisit each landmark in their relationship a spark of hope ignited, the flame flickering defiantly in the midst of her doubt she could ever be enough for him.

'*I want you to stay away from me,*' she'd lied.

'*You don't want that any more than I do,*' he'd replied.

Her heart tripped and picked up speed.

Unless he was trying to push her away Tyler didn't say things he didn't mean. But what if he'd been saying more than she'd heard? What if she'd been so wrapped up in how she felt—*for a change*—she'd missed how he felt?

She hadn't gone looking for it until she needed it to be there, but once she did…

'I'm supposed to keep my distance,' he'd said. But he couldn't do that any more than she could.

Surely that meant something—what if he felt the same draw to her that she felt to him?

He'd said when she had questions, *'You might want to make one of them why I kissed you the way I did…'*

What if everything she'd felt in that kiss hadn't come from her? She'd felt lost but he'd found her. She'd been hopeful but he'd lost hope. He'd said he was beyond saving. Did he really believe that—what if he thought *she* couldn't love *him* the way *he was?* He'd told her if he had a choice things would be different. *'Don't forget that.'*

Why had she forgotten that?

Even with her confidence battered by waves of fear and self-doubt the flame of hope continued to burn. The truth was she was more frightened of losing him than taking a leap of faith for the man she believed in more than she believed in herself. She'd thought he couldn't love her but if one day he *could...*

'When you figure it out let me know.'

Heart pounding rapidly, she jumped off the bed, grabbed the essentials and ran downstairs. Nothing on earth would stop her from going to him. She couldn't spend the rest of her life wondering what might have happened if she'd taken a chance. If the freedom she'd been dreaming of for her entire adult life was all about choice, then she chose *him.*

All he had to do was choose her back.

CHAPTER TWENTY-FIVE

HE *should* have kissed some sense into her. There was nothing wrong with his *mouth.*

But when Miranda was so nonchalant about never seeing him again it had knocked Tyler back. He couldn't even put on a damn T-shirt alone—how was he supposed to convince her that he would look after her for the rest of her life when he couldn't dress himself?

After a day spent fending off calls from his family, his partner, his captain, some moron from the press who wanted to paint him as a hero and a woman trying to sell him life insurance, Tyler paced the floor of his apartment like a caged animal. He reckoned Miranda had about twenty-four hours before he switched from the role of bodyguard to stalker. If he had to kidnap her and spend the next week demonstrating how much he wanted her then so be it. The physical pain he was experiencing from a couple of run-of-the-mill gunshot wounds was nothing compared to the agony he felt when he thought about losing her.

Now he'd risen from the ashes of his messed up life like the mythical phoenix of her code-name, he could plan a future. One he wanted to share with her.

But had he *told her that?*

He'd come to the sad conclusion he was a pathetic, cowardly weakling when there was a frantic knocking on the door of his apartment. At a little before midnight the last thing he expected on the other side was a breathless, wide-eyed Miranda. It was obviously raining again—the shoulders of her coat sparkling with silvery raindrops and her hair a shade darker. With her face flushed and devoid of make-up he thought she'd never looked more beautiful.

'Figured it out, did you?' he asked roughly.

Her brows wavered with uncertainty.

'Give it another minute.'

When she attempted to smile it wavered, too— her eyes shimmering with emotion as her breasts rose and fell with each rapid breath.

'Almost there…' The corner of his mouth lifted with the affection he didn't try to disguise.

Her smile was more convincing the second time,

growing in direct relation to the dawning realization in her eyes.

Tyler nodded. 'Took you long enough.'

As she made a sound halfway between a laugh and a sob he reached for her hand to draw her inside and kicked the door shut with his foot.

'Coat off.' He led her into the kitchen and jerked his chin at the counter. 'Sit up there. I'll be right back.'

When he returned from the bathroom with as many towels as he could carry in one hand she'd done what she was told without putting up a fight. That was a first.

'Why didn't you say something?' she asked.

Tyler tossed the towels down, selected one and stepped in front of her. 'When you were playing the role of Little Miss Don't-Give-A-Damn? Close your eyes.'

As she did he dried her face, her eyes opening again when he progressed to her hair.

'I was going to let you go.' The words were said in the small, vulnerable voice that turned him inside out.

'Too bad. I told you a while back—I'm in your life now. Get used to it.'

She blinked. 'Are you telling me you knew *then?*'

'No. I knew when you knocked me on my ass.'

'I knew when you kissed me on the ferry.'

He nodded. 'That's why you got scared.'

'Yes.' She frowned and reached for the towel. 'You shouldn't be doing that. You're hurt. I should be taking care of you. Not the other way around.'

Tyler allowed her to take it and watched as she set it aside. 'If we're gonna make this work there has to be a little of both—not that I'll make it easy for you.' His mouth curved into a wry smile. 'In case you hadn't got it already, I'm not a very good patient. I like to think I'm better at taking care of other people, if they'll let me.'

'No one's ever been there just for me,' she confessed. 'Not the way it felt you were in the last few weeks...'

'And that's never gonna change.' Not when it felt as if he'd been born to be with her. He watched as she blinked a tear from her lower lashes and dashed it away with the back of her hand. 'Can you tell me why you were scared?'

'It was too much and not enough.' She searched for a way to explain it. 'What your eyes were saying—I didn't want to hear if you were planning on walking away, but if you're not—'

'I'm *not,*' he stated firmly. 'But there are a couple of things we need to get straight before we go any further. Starting with your father.'

Her expression questioned where he was going.

'I won't let him fast-track me up the food chain to make me more suitable for you,' Tyler continued. 'When I get my career back on track it won't be for him, it'll be for us. I passed the sergeants exam six years ago—can ace the lieutenant one the same way, but when the time comes to aim higher if I hear so much as a rumour of whispers in the right ears there'll be trouble.'

She listened intently while tears filled her eyes but, as hard as they were to see, he couldn't stop to do anything about them until he'd said his piece. 'I'm an expert on interfering families—did some interfering of my own in return—so I know how it works. Being in love with his daughter doesn't make me a soft target for manipulation. He ever tries it with you again we'll be having words on the subject. You've sacrificed enough for the family business. From here on in your needs come first. It's already been tempting to tell your parents that to their faces. If they knew you the way I've started to—why are you smiling?'

It was bright enough to compete with the sun.

'You're in love with me?'

'That's the only thing you got from all that?'

'It's the only thing that matters.'

If it was they would never run into any problems but... 'Being a cop's wife isn't easy.'

Her eyes widened. 'You're proposing now?'

'I like to think when I'm proposing you'll know I'm doing it.' Nudging her knees apart to make space to step closer, he laid a possessive palm on her hip. 'What I'm saying is we've got time— take as much of it as you need and talk to as many members of my family as you want. I can't change who I am for you or keep you in the life-style you've been accustomed to but—'

She shook her head. 'You don't have to. I have money. That's not an issue.'

'It is if you think we're living off a trust fund.'

'It's not a trust fund. Well, it is until I turn twenty-five, but my parents didn't set it up. It's an inheritance from my grandfather.'

Tyler's eyes narrowed at the offhand tone to her voice. 'Are you telling me you're rich?'

'I'm afraid so. You'll have to learn to live with it.'

The words left his mouth before he could stop them. 'Even if it begs the question of what I can offer you?'

She ignored the question. 'You're *in love* with me?'

'Are you listening to anything I'm saying?'

'Yes.' She blinked a couple of times. 'I just seem to be a little stuck on that one...'

'Why?'

'I didn't think... I mean I thought I'd have to...' The uncharacteristic lack of something to say removed the frown from his face as she took a short breath. 'I haven't done anything to deserve it. I was awful to you at the start and then I was difficult. You were right—I'm hard work.'

'And I'm not?'

When he searched her eyes he found wonder mixed with the vulnerability she kept hidden from everyone else. Added to the insight he'd gained when she'd talked about her fear of not being enough, it felt as if the final piece of the puzzle had slotted into place. The need to reassure her made him reach out so he could hold her while he admitted there had been plenty of times she was more than he could handle. But when the sharp pain in his shoulder made him grit his teeth to stifle a groan a second possessive palm on her other hip was as close as he got.

'I'm no angel and I don't want to end up married to a saint, either.' He leaned closer. 'So if you think you have to be anything more than you already are you're wrong. You pulled me back from the edge. No one else could have done that. Last night—' he cleared his throat '—I went there to kill him.'

As he stood tall and waited for her judgment Miranda frowned. What was he talking about? Then it clicked. 'He was the guy you sent a message to.'

'Yes.'

Not that she believed it for a second. 'Why were you going to kill him?'

'He made it personal.'

'How?'

His gaze lowered to one of her hands when she set them on his forearms. 'Her name was Candice.'

Miranda felt an immediate surge of jealousy.

'I busted her a few times when I was with Vice.'

She exhaled the breath she was holding.

'When she fed me some useful pieces of information I put her on the payroll—one of them led to a drugs bust that took me to Narcotics.' He took a long, controlled breath. 'A month before I got assigned to Municipal Security her dealer changed and she witnessed something that could have put a major player behind bars. I said I'd protect her if she agreed to give evidence in court but left her alone to chase the lead. By the time I got back she was dead.'

'What happened?'

'He beat her to death with a baseball bat.' The hand at the end of his good arm moved from her hip to tunnel underneath her sweater in a way that suggested he needed to feel the warmth of her skin. 'I recruited her. I ignored the danger she was in and it got her killed. To him it was business. To me it was personal.'

With the explanation, how seriously he'd taken *her* safety made perfect sense to Miranda. She ran a palm up his arm, across his shoulder and raised it to his jaw, waiting for him to look into her eyes before she spoke. 'I know you well enough to know if you thought something might happen to her you would never have left her alone. You'd have fought for her, Tyler—taken the beating for her if you could, died if it meant saving her life.'

While trying to bring her murderer to justice he almost had.

'I should have known the risk.'

'If you think worst-case scenario in every situation…' The realization it was exactly what he'd been doing twisted her heart. 'That's why you saw potential threats everywhere you looked when you became my bodyguard, isn't it?'

'Partly,' he admitted reluctantly, before pressing

his mouth into a thin line. 'If I tell you something you have to promise not to freak out.'

Meaning she wasn't going to like it…

'The guy outside the movie theatre was the one I saw outside the school.' Long fingers flexed against her skin in reassurance. 'Lewis Rand was briefed but I need you to be careful until I track down the rest of the letter writers. There's only a couple more to go so—'

'Wait.' She interrupted. 'Are you talking about Paul?'

He frowned. 'Who the hell is Paul?'

'Dark hair, glasses, has a problem with the three-second handshake rule.'

'You *know him?*'

Miranda nodded. 'He's a self-professed super-fan. Re-Tweets everything I say on Twitter and tries to see me in the real world as often as he can. He's quite sweet really. His mother died a few years ago and I think he's lonely.'

'Great,' Tyler said flatly. 'I threatened Bambi.'

'You can apologize the next time you see him. If we get married he'll probably be outside the church…'

'*If* we get married?'

'We'll get to that in a minute.' Sliding her hand from his jaw to the back of his neck, she wriggled closer to the edge of the counter and locked her legs around the backs of his knees. 'Tell me about last night.'

'I couldn't take the shot.'

'Because you're not a murderer,' she said firmly.

'I wasn't sure any more. Was starting to forget who I was until I met you...' A corner of his mouth lifted to form another wry smile. 'It was part of the reason I told myself I couldn't sleep with you. Believe me when I say it had squat to do with not wanting you.' As if to prove the point his hand moved, the tip of his thumb grazing the lace on the underside of her breast while his eyes darkened. 'I got hooked with dance moves—wanted to take you hard and fast in the hall that night. There isn't a single inch of your body I don't want to kiss.' When his smile changed the returning hint of predator sent a sizzle of heat through her veins. 'You're gonna be spending a lot of time naked.'

Miranda blinked, consumed by the hunger in his eyes. 'You're wounded...'

The protest sounded unconvincing, even to her.

'I'm not *that* wounded,' he replied with conviction. 'Where you are right now works for me— or you on top, that would work, too... I've had a mental image of that one for a while now.'

Not that it had ever taken much but in a heartbeat her body was ready for him, the squirming movement she made on the counter creating a knowing gleam in his eyes.

'And now you're picturing it, aren't you?'

'I have a lot of those mental images,' she confessed. 'But before we start swapping them, I should warn you being the husband of a politician's daughter won't be easy.'

'*If* we get married?' he repeated in a lower, rougher, unbelievably seductive voice.

'You haven't proposed yet,' she pointed out as she ran her fingertips over the short hair at the back of his neck. 'What I'm saying is we've got time for you to ease into it. Knowing my father, he'll run for governor in a few years and when he does we'll be asked to stand onstage with him to show our support.'

'You'll still do that?'

'Not full time.'

'Gonna have to vote for him, aren't I?' Tyler asked as he focused his intense gaze on her mouth and leaned closer.

The tip of her tongue flicked over her lips. 'I won't tell if you don't. I'm Team Tyler all the way.'

'No, you're not. We're Team Us.' He stilled and leaned back to look into her eyes. 'At least we would be if you'd ever get around to saying you love me back.'

She fluttered her eyelashes in response. 'You hadn't figured it out already?'

When he raised his hand from her hip the grimace of pain was impossible to hide.

'What are you doing?'

'I'm moving into position to kiss it out of you. It's just not gonna be with this hand.'

'When's the last time you took pain meds?'

Lowering his bad arm, he freed the hand beneath her sweater so he could push aside damp tendrils of hair and wrap long fingers around the nape of her neck. 'Kissing you will take my mind off it.'

Before he turned her brain to mush Miranda framed his face in her hands and looked deep into his eyes so he could hear her loud and clear. 'Of course I love you. How could I not? I believe in you more than I've ever believed in anyone. I may have questioned why but it never felt wrong. The only thing that did was fighting how I felt.'

Something endearingly close to relief crossed his eyes before they darkened to the colour of stormy seas. 'That guy you talked about finding when you have your freedom—the one who'll spend time with you because he wants to and not because he's paid to do it? *It's me.*'

The depth of emotion he projected with his eyes combined with the strength of conviction in his deep voice removed any lingering doubt she had left about being enough for him. He wouldn't love her that much, want her that badly or bare his soul to someone he considered unworthy.

'It feels like I belong here,' she said in a voice thick with the same depth of emotion. 'There's something about you that makes me want to hold on and never let go. When I thought this was over—'

'We're just getting started,' he argued. 'You can make me angrier than any woman I've ever known but I'd still rather fight with you than make love with anyone else.'

'Ooh…that was *good*…' She raised her brows. 'Do you have more of those?'

When he laughed it was the most glorious, uplifting sound she'd ever heard. 'You have no idea how much I wanted to hear that again. You have a great laugh. You should do it more often.'

'You know you're not going home tonight, right?'

'I *am* home.' She tore her gaze away to flick a brief glance over his shoulder. 'But you might need more closet space before I move in. Wow. You have a lot of books.'

A light kiss was placed on the corner of her mouth. 'I like to read.'

'You can't have read all of them.'

'Yes, I can, and you could sound less surprised.' He bestowed another kiss on her eager lips. 'What's more I remember them word for word. You can pick a page later.'

Miranda felt the heat coiling low in her abdomen. 'You have a photographic memory?'

'The term is didactic and I plan to rewrite the rules by filling my memory with images of you. The look on your face when I propose...' Kiss. 'How beautiful you are when you walk down the aisle...' Kiss. 'When you hold our first child...' Kiss. 'Wiping away your tears when we attend their graduation...' Kiss. 'We're gonna make a lifetime of memories and when it's my time I'll take every one of them with me and die a happy man.'

The demonstration of how much he'd been holding back created a swell of emotion it was impossible to contain, joy leaking from the corners of her closed eyes as she leaned her forehead against his. 'I love you *so much*.'

'And I love you. Don't ever doubt that.' He

leaned back and waited for her to open her eyes before adding, 'Still questioning what I did to deserve you but I reckon I've got at least sixty years to figure it out.'

When he winked, Miranda grinned. He was all the fun she would ever need. As he went to work with remarkable one-handed dexterity on the buttons down the centre of her sweater she answered his question in a way that made perfect sense to a woman whose childhood belief in happily-ever-after had been renewed.

'That's the thing about rescuing the princess from her ivory tower.' She kissed his crooked smile. 'Once he does, the hero of the story is kinda stuck with her after that.'

* * * * *